BOUGHT

by the

MAFIA

PIPER KNOX

LETTER B

This is a work of fiction. Names, characters, places, and incidents either are the product of the author's imagination or are used fictitiously. Any resemblance to actual persons, living or dead, events, or locales is entirely coincidental.

Copyright © 2023 by Piper Knox

All rights reserved. No part of this book may be reproduced or used in any manner without written permission of the copyright owner except for the use of quotations in a book review. For more information, address: pipercknox@gmail.com.

First paperback edition August 2023

ISBN: 9798856746012

Published by Letter B Press

OTHER BOOKS IN THIS SERIES

THE MAFIA'S CAPTIVE

THE MAFIA'S PROPERTY

OTHER BOOKS BY PIPER KNOX

Manhattan Kings Duet

THE REVENGE PLAN

THE FAKE DATING PLAN

BOUGHT BY THE MAFIA

1

SIMONA

The wedding was a quick affair. Some might even call it hasty. As soon as it was arranged, the date was set; the venue was picked, and I was getting married. Everything was done for me and all I had to do was show up. I didn't even pick my wedding dress. My father chose, or rather, he hired a shopping assistant and gave her strict instructions not to buy anything 'a whore might wear.' His words, not mine. As for the groom, he too was a pick out of my hands. A man from one of the most powerful families in the world. Well, our world, at least. The Morelli name was not that well known to anyone on the street, but it carried weight in the criminal underground and I'd just become one of them.

The whole arranged marriage thing wouldn't have been so bad if I didn't know him and he didn't know me. But I seem to have a phobia of good luck. My new husband hated me, and I hated him just as much. A match made in hell. It's a wonder we could keep it civil throughout the wedding. Marrying a Morelli was the only good thing I had done so far in my father's eyes, and I think that was what made me endure the ceremony. The pride in my father's eyes was enough to dampen the disdain in my husband's.

I looked down at the big diamond ring on my finger. Surreal did not even begin to describe how I was feeling. I'm a married woman now. A married woman driving to a new home in an unfamiliar city. I looked at the man who had put the ring. Giovanni Morelli was incredibly handsome. Time had graced him with its artistry, like Michelangelo. The boyish softness that made him appear sweet the last I met him was now hardened into chiseled features that made him both irresistible and dangerous. He was a beautiful man, but his best feature by far were his eyes. They were deep pools of black, the color only rivaled by his equally dark hair.

My cousin, a daughter of my father's capo who had been rushed into becoming my bridesmaid, had said, "You're so lucky." The others had agreed. They were all enamored with him. If only they knew the truth. A father exchanging his daughter for a proximity to power could not be a good thing.

"What?"

I jumped. Did I stare too long? I scrambled to think of something. "Are we there yet?" Just as I finished saying that, the car slowed down and parked in front of an Upper East Side apartment building.

"We're here," Gio said. His tone was glib and abrupt. He had been like that throughout the wedding. He never spoke no more than three words to me. And it wasn't because he was reserved or anything. With other people, he was downright talkative. Just not to me.

His bodyguards, two bulky men whose names I hadn't caught yet, got out of the front of the car and opened both our doors. Gio got out first and didn't wait for me. I practically had to run up to him so I can keep up with his long strides and only caught up just as we entered the elevator. He typed in a code and we were whisked up the building. The doors opened to what I assumed was the penthouse. A palatial apartment with tasteful white, black and dark brown decor, floor-to-ceiling windows and a spiral staircase that led to a second floor. Everything in the apartment, from the vase to the artwork on the walls, was a quiet statement of wealth. The Morellis had not only gotten powerful since the last time I was within their air, they've gotten filthy rich as well. I looked around the foyer, living room, terrace, and kitchen. Gio noticed me gawking.

"Like what you see?" he said.

"Your place is beautiful." My voice came out strained from being quiet during the long trip.

He smirked. It was as if I said what he expected me to say, and it was the wrong thing to say. I wanted to ask why he thought that, but I knew the truth already. Having him spell it out would only lead to pain. He marched into the apartment towards the staircase. "Let me show you to your room," he said without sparing a glance to see if I will follow him. I did anyway and had to scurry just to keep up with his long strides. I was moving so fast I almost bumped into him when, abruptly, he stopped at a door. He opened to reveal a bedroom. He entered, and I followed. It was not just a bedroom, but a suite. There was a bed on one end and a living space with a small table and plush stools on the other end. Mirrored doors led to a large closet, and a bathroom with a tub facing the city skyline. "Yours," he said after the quick tour. As he left the room, I peered behind him to where another bedroom with a door slightly ajar was located. If the dark gray and black decor I could see from beyond was anything to go by, "mine" was opposite his. It was in stark contrast to the delicate white, pink accents and gold in my bedroom.

"Don't worry," he said when he saw me glaring. "I won't be accosting you in the middle of the night. Or any other time of day. Whatever passion I held for you cooled a long time ago."

I felt a piercing in my heart. His barbs should have been blunt against my barricade and, in fact, I felt the same as he did, but they hurt still. That week we spent together should be a wisp of a memory now that five years had passed, however I would be lying to myself if I said I didn't think about him now and then. Did that mean I was still obsessed? No. So why would it bother me he had forgotten it as well? "Why did you marry me then?" I said.

He folded his arms. "I thought you knew this was an arranged marriage, whose sole purpose was for me to get your father's alliance. Didn't he tell you? If you thought otherwise—"

"I know that! But there are other families you

could have approached. Families within this city even."

His gaze bore into me and for a moment I thought he wasn't going to answer until he said, "We wanted old blood and their connections. Your family was more than sufficient."

"We? You and your brothers?"

He shrugged.

The Morelli family was famous for being run by the four Morelli brothers after their father died. According to my father, the brothers had taken the family from being relatively small to one of the biggest Mafia families in the country and, frankly, the world. Big enough to make my usually snobbish, blood-obsessed father dance with glee at the prospect of having his daughter marry into them.

"Still doesn't explain it. Why us and not any other old blood family?"

"Our reasoning was pure calculation, Simona. You becoming my bride is simply a coincidence. You were supposed to marry Dante, but he ended up entangled with someone else."

The someone else must be the woman Dante was with at the wedding. They seemed wrapped in a cocoon of love no one could pierce.

"So you would have married anyone else if wasn't me." I raised my eyebrows.

He shrugged again.

"Liar."

"What? Surprised to find out that you're not that special? Sorry to break it to you, but there are other things I wanted more and you're merely collateral."

"I know what you're trying to do."

"And what is that?"

"You're trying to break me. Put me in what you must assume is my place. But I'm not going to be bothered by your antics for as long as this marriage last."

"Last I checked, marriage was a forever thing. Till death do us part. Isn't that what the vows you recited said?"

"Yes, but…" I shifted my weight. Suddenly, the heels I was wearing felt too steep and clunky. "There's going to be a divorce, right?" I spurted a laughter. "You can't expect me to be married to you forever."

"Looks like someone didn't read the fine print," he said and strode out further into the corridor. I followed him, doing that running-marching thing again to keep up with him. "I'm not doing this forever."

"But that's the deal you signed Simona," he said as he went down the stairs. His two bodyguards were entering the apartment carrying suitcases, most of them mine, and placing them on top of others.

"You can put them in Simona's bedroom, Mike," Gio said to one of them, who nodded. And the other guy followed the first guy's lead as they passed me by one their way up. If this was any other time, I would be worried about two men handling my things, but this was different. My husband, who I had assumed was only going to be a temporary husband, was now telling me this thing was permanent. When I spoke to father, when I agreed to the deal, he assured me it would only be temporary. Five years at most. Two if the whole business with their 'enemies' was decided early. "Besides," father had said, "He could die in this war they're fighting before the five years is done. You could become a rich widow."

"That's not what I agreed to."

He still wasn't looking at me. I felt like I was a nuisance he could barely register. I watched him as he went over to the living room bar and poured himself a dark golden liquid. "Take it up with your father. He's the one who insisted. Kids too, he said. I had to renege on that one."

He took a sip of the drink and finally faced me. And a lot fell into place. This was his plan. He had planned all of this. His smile, which he couldn't hide as he drank his brandy, said everything. And my father. My father had willingly deceived me into marrying a man I hated.

"Why would you do this? Why you would tie yourself to someone who hates you and guaranteed to make your life miserable?"

"That's the thing, isn't it? I'm guaranteed to make *your* life miserable."

It was my turn to smirk. "So you still haven't forgotten."

His smile died. He placed his drink at the bar and stalked over to where I was standing and gripped my chin. Fear took hold of me. Fear and something else. My gaze fell on the opening of his shirt, bringing back memories of me running my hands over his chest. I raised my gaze to the lips that had once kissed mine with passion and ardor. The something else was lust, I realized. I held his gaze in defiance so he would not know whatever I felt. Be it fear or longing.

"I never said I've forgotten Mona. Only that I never want to touch you again."

I dared not point out the irony of that statement. "Funny how you still hold a grudge after all these years over something so trivial."

His grip on my chin tightened. "You almost ruined my life with that silly little thing you pulled. You almost upended a business with your little tricks. Forgive me if I feel a little vengeful over it."

I know what I did. It was bad and some might even say unforgivable, but to say it derailed a business was going overboard. "You sound a little dramatic."

He glared at me one more time and let go of my chin like it was a hot piece of iron. And went back to the bar, where he chugged the rest of his drink. "The point is, you're mine to do whatever I want with, whenever I want, however I want."

"And if I say no? Don't think I would let you bully me and take it. I'm going to fight back, and I will divorce you after your little war is over."

"I wouldn't be so sure about that last part."

"What have you got? Give me your best shot."

"How about your mother?"

I froze. My mother was currently at a center recovering from multiple addictions for what feels like the first time in a long time. Our relationship was finally back on track and everything was going well. If Gio was thinking of doing something to her, he did not know what hell I would unleash. "What have you done with my mother?"

"Nothing yet. But I doubt your father knows where she is, does he?"

"Where are you going with this?"

"If he knew, I can only imagine what he would

do to her. I heard your parents have had a contentious relationship, in marriage and out of it."

"Don't you dare."

"Then there's the whole money aspect. Two million was it she stole from him? Or was it more than that? I can't recall. The apple didn't fall very far, did it?"

Gio was no longer the boy I once knew. He was a force capable of doing harm to me and to the people I care for. He could destroy me if he wanted. I wasn't going to let that happen. "What do you want?" My voice shook as I spoke, the realization slowly sinking in. "H-how did you know? To find her. How did you find her?"

"Don't worry, your father doesn't know… yet. But who knows what will happen when he finds out?"

"Please." I rushed over to him. "Please don't let him know. I'll do whatever you say." I hated this position he had put me in, but I would do everything to protect my mother, flawed as she was, she was still the woman who brought me into this world. Giovanni knew my weakness, and he had exploited it perfectly.

I heard someone clearing their throat behind me and saw that the two men had finished moving the luggage. Funny how I hadn't heard them all this time. "You can leave," Gio said to them.

"Right on, boss," the one called Mike said. As they were leaving, Giovanni poured another drink in his glass and another one, which he handed to me. I downed half of the fiery liquid like a thirsty woman in a desert.

Gio could not help himself. He looked like a self-satisfied Cheshire cat. Happy in my misery. How did he even find my mother? I was so sure the rehab I sent her to was in a remote area and far different from where most of the people I knew usually went.

"Does that mean you're ready to play ball?"

I nodded. What other choice did I have?

He motioned to sit on one of the living room sofas. I perched myself onto one, ready to hear what was coming next. Whatever it was, it could not be good. He sat down opposite me. I took another sip of the brandy.

"Now that we're on the same page, I thought we should lay a few ground rules. It's something I should have done before the wedding, but I was a little busy."

"I'm listening."

"First; now that you're my wife, a Morelli, you are expected to behave in a certain way. That means no more partying. Especially with those friends of yours."

I split with "those friends" of mine a long time

ago after my father cut me off and they realized they couldn't mooch of me anymore, so that wasn't much of an issue. But he couldn't expect me to stay couped up in here. No matter how lovely his place was. "I am not even invited to parties anymore? I should reject all of those? No more birthday parties, bridal showers, work parties?"

"About that, second; put in your resignation."

"Now that's something I won't be doing."

"I thought you said you will play along. Your father is only one call away. I could easily tell him where your mother is."

"But I love my job! What do you expect me to do with my life?"

"A good and dutiful wife. Third; you can't have any boyfriends none what so ever."

"And if I'm horny? It's not like you're going to satisfy me."

His eyes flared. "Use a dildo."

"And what about you? Will you be using a fleshlight, or does the man get to have mistresses?"

"If you want me to be faithful, I'll stay faithful."

The compromise came out of nowhere and cooled some of the anger that was building and made me bolder. "If I can't get any, you can't get any."

"Fine by me. That's it. Those are the only rules. Obey those and you and I will not have any issues.

"Except I haven't agreed to the second rule. I am going to work, regardless if you like it or not."

"You not working at that company is non-negotiable."

"So you have an issue with me working at that place in particular? Why?"

He held his head in his hands. "Why are you so determined to make this hard?"

"Why are you so eager to turn me into a housewife? Whatever fetish you have of me, I'm sorry I'm not going to cater to it."

"Do I need to remind you that you're not in a position to negotiate?" If I quit my job, I might as well tell my father where mom was. My job was the only way I could keep her at the rehab center. If I lose that, I lose her. Again. And there was no way I was going to ask Gio for money.

"I don't care. I won't quit my job."

"Why do you love it so much? Aren't you like a seamstress there or something?"

"I'm actually a stylist." And if I worked hard enough, they could promote me to deputy creative director. I had a genuine career path there. I wasn't going to let it go.

"Funny that you care about it. But sadly no. Resign tomorrow. Those are the terms."

"I hate you."

"Back at you babe."

And he left.

2

GIOVANNI

She was testing my patience. That had to be it. Otherwise, why refuse to resign from her frivolous job, even though she was married to a multi-millionaire? Billionaire, if you counted the off-shore assets. It was two weeks since we got married and still; she hadn't left her job.

A cold war was waging in my home, and it was draining me. I would say she should do something, just one thing, and she would not refuse, but simply not do it. I would remind her, and she would acknowledge the reminder and then forget about it. She must have realized by now that I wasn't ready to deploy the "expose your mother's location" nuke, thus emboldening her. Instead of leaving earlier than I for work, she was simply leaving the same time as I was, as if daring me to do something.

Problem is, she did not know how she was endangering the business with her stupid standoff. It was just as well that she didn't know the consequences of her actions, otherwise she would have used it against me.

I should have been concentrating on my work, but I was instead wasting my brain power thinking about Simona and her stupid antics. Graphs, words, and numbers were floating on my laptop screen like a jumble of undecipherable financial data. Even when my phone chimed, the noise felt louder than usual and pulled me out of my pretend concentration. It was her. And she was testing me further by sending this asinine text. The nerve. The gal to send a text like that. I thought of calling her father. Not to do what I had threatened, that was something I wouldn't do even to someone I hated like Simona, but maybe to return the goods and ask for a refund? Her father was a well-known violent man and who knew how he would retaliate towards her? I had some sympathy for Simona. A little, not a lot, but her insolence had to end. Simona had cost my business once. I would not let her cost us again.

I put in a call. The phone rang and rang until I thought the call was going to die, when she picked it up. "You saw my message?" she said on the other end. Talking to her over the phone was just as devastating as talking to her in person. Her voice had a sultry quality enough to drive any virile man insane. It was equally matched by her stunning beauty, which had made me speechless the first time I saw her after five years. It did not differ from when I first met her. Amazing how she still could shut down my voice box.

"Hello?" I heard her say on the other end. Like a love-struck teenager, I had gone quiet again. I felt a lump in my throat and cleared it. "You should hand in your resignation, not go to Paris."

"You don't control me." The line went dead.

Why did she keep insisting on making everything difficult? If Dante were to find out that my wife was working for a Saccone money-laundering front, he would have my head. The twins would not stop him. Wouldn't they love reminding me it wasn't the first time I sabotaged the business? There was no way I was going to let that happen again, which meant there was only one thing to do. Drag her out of there myself.

The offices weren't that far away. A five-minute drive at the back of my town car and I was there. The place looked like what one would expect a typical fashion magazine office space to look like. White marble walls, abstract art, and framed magazine covers. Skinny white girls scurrying in heels. My presence as soon as I got into the reception attracted a lot of attention. The two receptionists glared at me as soon as the elevator doors opened. A few of the people sitting in the lobby looked up from their phones. The girls would glance at me and my three bodyguards in perplexed amusement as they ran past. It had the desired effect. The receptionist I approached looked similarly petrified when I asked her I wanted to see the editor-in-chief.

"Um, d-do you have an appointment?"

"Tell her it's Giovanni Morelli. She'll make time."

She dialed a number and spoke to the girl on the other end of the call she made and then said, "A-apparently she's in a meeting."

"Tell the assistant to tell her boss that Giovanni Morelli is here."

She peered at me for five long seconds, clearly conflicted about whether she should push back or do as I say. The latter won, and she called back.

A few minutes later, a smartly dressed short

woman with silver black streaked hair came marching in. "Gio," with a hand extended, "to what do I owe this marvelous surprise?"

"Judy." I said, accepting her greeting. "I had a minor issue I wanted to discuss with you, nothing pertinent," I replied and followed as she led me to her offices. I signaled my men to stay in the lobby, much to the chagrin of the receptionist, who kept peering at them from behind the counter.

When we arrived at her office, I saw the receptionist was indeed telling the truth. She was in a meeting. Albeit a staff meeting with three other employees, one of them who was my wife. Simona bolted from her chair when she saw me coming in. "Let's reschedule this later girls, I have company," Judy said to them.

"Except for Simona," I said. Everyone looked at both her and me with curious glances. Ah, this was going to be interesting. Judy seemed just as perplexed as she told Simona to remain. I took a chair beside Simona. Her hands were shaking, I noticed. With fear or anger? I could not tell.

"Sorry to bother you on such a busy day," I said to Judy.

She dismissed my apology with a flicker of the wrist. "Oh, it's nothing at all. You know you're welcome to walk in and out whenever you like.

What I want to know is how you two know each other?"

I frowned. "She didn't tell you? Seems like my wife is not as excited as I am about our marriage."

Judy's eyes bulged. "Married!" She turned her gaze to Simona. "Simona! When? Where? Why didn't you tell us?"

"I've been meaning to," Simona said in a low voice before glaring at me. She looked like she wanted to punch me in the gut. It was definitely anger that was making her shake. Good. That I can handle. I glanced down at her hand and noticed something else that was off. Raising Simona's hand and showing it to Judy I said, "I don't think so. Looks like you didn't want your coworkers to know. Where's your ring, darling?"

"It, um, kept slipping off. It looks really expensive, and I didn't want to lose it." Like the consummate liar she is, the excuse came out smoothly.

"But why didn't you tell us! And when did this happen?"

"A couple of weeks ago in Tuscany," I responded.

"And you didn't think to invite us! Simona!"

"Please don't blame her. I insisted on the whole affair being intimate and close family only for security."

Judy understood my meaning and leaned back in her chair. "Of course."

"But my nuptials are not why I'm here. Well, it's connected." I took Simona's hand in my lap. "Simona and I had both planned on Simona taking some time off while she got to fixing up our new home. My place right now screams man and would do with some redecorating, and Simona wanted to do it full time."

"Aww," Judy said.

"Whatever my wife wants, my wife gets. It can look like a hello kitty doll threw up in there and it would still be fine as long as she likes it. But before we did all that, I wanted to take her on a honeymoon first. The Maldives maybe, but we haven't decided. The romance was a bit of a whirlwind and the wedding was quick, but I really want to do the honeymoon justice."

"Well, of course. Again, why didn't you tell me? You've been working hard girl, you deserve a break."

A tight smile spread across Simona's face. "I know, but with Paris and everything, I couldn't just leave."

Judy waved her off. "Please. We will manage here. They say the early days of marriage are the best days. Trust me, you don't want to spend most of them at work."

"That's exactly what I told her." Simona squeezed my hand.

"And if you want to take an indefinite leave, you can," Judy said. This was going better than I could hope for. "Your job will be there whenever you come back."

"But the scheduled shoots."

"Fleur will take care of that."

"And the dresses."

"We can always find a replacement," Judy said. "None better than you, but like your handsome piece of hunk husband said, you deserve a nice break."

"Starting now even," I said.

Judy laughed. "Starting now!"

Simona squeezed my hand so tight; I thought a finger would pop off. But it didn't matter. I had won this round. Judy made a few calls and a few minutes later, we were at the elevator where she was giving us well wishes and bidding both of us goodbye. She even promised to send Simona's stuff to the apartment.

When the doors closed, I felt a sharp sting on my cheek. "You bastard," Simona said after slapping me.

"What? I got you out of a job from a failing company in a dying industry. You should thank me, really."

"That was my livelihood!"

"Not since you married me. You have an allowance."

"My career will be ruined!"

"She said your job will be there whenever you decide to return."

"You think you have an answer for everything, don't you?"

"I don't have the answer to why you keep taunting me every time. I told you to resign. You answer by telling me you're going out of the country for work. How was I supposed to react?"

"By not taking my job away, you oaf!"

"Actually, now that I remember, your job will not be there in a few weeks, anyway. You might as well thank me. But you're free to work somewhere else."

Her eyes narrowed. "What do you mean 'Your job won't be there in a few weeks.' And by the way," she folded her arms, "How do you and Judy know each other?"

The elevator came to a stop at that moment and opened the doors to the parking lot. My other bodyguard, Lex, had already gone down and had the car ready for us. "Me and Judy go way back," I said, offering my hand to help her get in the car. She ignored it and entered on her own. I followed her. "The Morelli fund was the first investor in the company back in the eighties. I recouped the investment when I took the reins of the investment firm, but we've been on good terms."

She smirked. "So, after all this time, you knew where I was working. You seem to be more interested in me than I thought."

"I never gave you the time of day, Simona, no matter how much your narcissistic brain like to imagine yourself as the center of the world."

She whipped her head away from me and turned her entire body towards the door, suddenly finding the passing city appealing. The dig hit its intended target, but it was not true. I *had* thought about her ever since we last met. Hell, I only found out Judy and Saccone were connected through a brief background check I did before we got married. An occupational hazard. This led me to learning more about Judy's recent financial straits and that she had gone to Saccone for help. And all the while, I couldn't help but wonder if Simona had any connection to it. Thankfully, she was just as oblivious to what her boss was doing as was most of the workforce at that company.

I tried to stop thinking of her, but I could not. Pictures of her in a blue swimsuit kept popping up in my head whenever my mind wandered, followed by dirtier thoughts. Other images came as well. Images of her betrayal. Memories of her treachery, and then I would remember her chest hid a void were a heart should be. She could not fool me. I had to remain vigilant about what my new wife was capable of. That is why I had to keep her close. I could not care less what she did, but she had to do it where I could see her. She had ruined me once. She could do it again. I wasn't going to let that happen again.

3

SIMONA

Five years ago

A familiar musical tone took me out of my warm sleep and instantly ruining the peaceful moment I was having. The once cute kitten-meowing ringtone was getting more irritating ever since I came to Santorini. I closed my eyes again and willed my phone to stop. Maybe if I don't cut and let it ring, she'll think I'm not near my phone. Maybe she'll stop calling.

"Is it not important?"

I opened my eyes again and this time, a man stood in front of me, blocking the sun. A very handsome shade, a random thought of mine suggested. He looked local, but sounded American. He was in his trunks and stood with a casual confidence that I've seen few pull off. It was easier for him with the type of body he had. Washboard abs and lean muscles on a tall frame. And then there was his face, chiseled cheekbones, deep black eyes hooded by thick eyelashes. Maybe I was still asleep and dreaming of a Greek god. I was on a Greek island, after all.

"You should put in on vibrate at least if you don't want to pick it up."

I turned to my phone just as the ringing ended and then back to him. A blush spread all over my body as I realized I was ogling. "I'm sorry, was it too irritating?"

"I don't mind hearing a cat meowing, but when it happens endlessly for—"

The phone rang again. I picked it up with a renewed sense of embarrassment. "Sorry," I muttered as I put the phone on vibrate. "There, now you can enjoy your holiday in peace."

I was sure this was going to be our last conversation, and if we were ever to meet again, it would be at a distance or at the breakfast buffet, but it wasn't. Far from it. This was our fateful encounter.

"I don't think that will be possible after now," he said.

Oh no. It seemed like I had made the Greek god hate me. Just my luck. "Please don't tell me I've just ruined your afternoon."

"Quite the opposite actually," he said, sitting down on the chaise next to mine. I looked around. There were a smattering of people on the beach, and a lot more unoccupied chairs than occupied. His choosing to sit next to me was deliberate. My pulse beat a little faster. "I was looking for company, but if you don't want to talk…"

"Oh no, it's fine," I said, sitting upright. "We can talk."

"I'll start. Who's calling you? Not a boyfriend, husband or lover, I hope?"

It was my mother actually. "None of the above."

He smiled the most heart-warming smile. The type that made a woman forgive a man all the bad he's done. This is dangerous. He was dangerous, and if I wasn't careful, he was going to make this week that much more tough. A distraction was the last thing I needed.

Now

This was my punishment. That was the only explanation. Otherwise, why would he take away my only source of joy? He wasn't over Santorini as much as he acted like the past was behind him. He was going to use this marriage to punish me. This act of cruelty was proof.

After he dropped me off at the apartment and posting one of his big and scary bodyguards by the door, he drove off to work and left me fuming and pacing, until my legs were tired. Then I sat fuming until I tired of being angry. Slowly, though, my rage got replaced with retribution. I wasn't going to let him bully me, just because he had an upper hand in this marriage. I had to strike back. But before I could think of how I was going to exact vengeance of my own, I heard him enter. I looked outside, and it was already nighttime. The moment he entered the room, my breath hitched in my throat. Despite our history, my body still reacted to him like it was the first time. The loose tie and unbuttoned collar did not help. My gaze was immediately drawn to that spot that showed part of his chest. Focus. Remember what he did to you.

"Surprised you didn't run away while I was gone?"

"You know what's stopping me."

He smirked. "There's a good girl. Doing what

she's told. You have grown, it seems."

I rolled my eyes and stood up. "It doesn't mean I'm no longer angry at you. Or that I'm actually behaving, as you say. I still want my job back."

"Sorry. Can't have it."

"Then say goodbye to your marriage."

"Are you forgetting something? Or should I say someone? One phone call to your father—"

"And I can just as easily make a call to your brother. Dante is it? He's the older one, right? I could let me see," I looked up at the ceiling, feigning calculation, "tell him you and I were fighting."

His face became hard. "What are you getting at?"

"When you left me, instead of thinking of ways to get out, I thought of other ways. I know for a fact that this marriage benefits the Morelli family and whatever your reasons for revenge, you married me because you had to, or your brother told you to. I don't care. But do you know what your brother told me at the wedding?"

He smirked and his voice was low when he said, "I'm dying to know."

He seemed surprised by this revelation, but he didn't show it. I had to tread carefully. "He said, 'if my brother gives you any trouble, call me and I will end it.' I thought it was a cute promise but he seemed serious. And I was just thinking I could take him up on that offer. It wouldn't be very hard to fake a minor bruise. I can even hit myself if I have to."

He stalked over to where I was standing until we were a few inches away from each other. I should have been scared. There was barely controlled anger radiating from him, and it threatened to come out. "You wouldn't dare."

"Try me, you son of a bitch. What? Do you want to make it real? You want to punch me? Go ahead."

His fists clenched and unclenched. I stood my ground. It's not like I would go through with framing him. But he thought me to be the worst human on earth, so why disabuse him of that notion? As long as he doesn't call my bluff, he would assume I have a trigger button of my own and that made us equal.

"Do you really want that job badly?"

"Weren't you the one who once said I should do something meaningful with my life instead of partying? Well, here I am."

"You can't have that job. But," he took a deep breath, "you can do something else. Different or otherwise. You could start your own magazine for all I care, as long as you don't go back there. I can even be your angel investor. I can give you a million dollars clean."

It was my turn to be surprised. "You would do that for me?"

"It would not be for you."

Of course. It was for his preservation, not because of anything he saw in me. "Why don't you want me working there, anyway?"

"It's none of your business."

"It is the mafia, isn't it?"

"Again, none of your business."

Gears started turning in my head. I recalled Judy getting stressed last year, cutting costs, and claiming she was going to start layoffs soon. Then, only a few months later, all that stress was gone. In fact, we were planning on going to Paris fashion week, something that would have been a fantasy last year. I figured it was because the magazine was more profitable than before, but what if she found another source? "Oh, my god. Judy is using mafia money to boost her business, isn't she?"

He scoffed. "You've never lacked brains; I'll give you that."

"Your mafia money?"

"Cute, but I deal with the legal side of the family business. And besides, she's a friend. I would never use her to launder our money."

"But someone else is? Did you blackmail her?"

"Didn't need to."

"Your enemy then. That's why you don't want me working there?"

This time, he didn't respond. Not even with a snark, but I knew I was right. It was all over his face. He looked as if he couldn't believe I worked it out. "Why didn't you just tell me?"

"That's because our relationship is on a need-to-know basis."

"Fine. I'll take the money, as long as it's clean, and I won't ask any more questions."

"It's not as simple as that, though."

"What are you getting at?"

His eyes flared. "You're going to have to earn it."

"How? You want me to work for you or something?"

"Something like that." Gio's gaze dropped to my chest. The white blouse I had on was low cut and revealed a little cleavage. His naked glare made me feel like I had my boobs bared. When I grasped his meaning, heat crept up my cheeks. He wanted to fuck me for it. The idea held appeal, as much as I hated to admit it, but what would he think of me if I said yes? Did his opinion of me even matter?

"I'm not your whore," I said.

"Some might disagree, but I don't care how

you label yourself. But you're my wife."

"I thought you didn't want to touch me."

"I don't. But apparently, I must," he said.

My eyes narrowed. "What are you getting at?"

"Your brother called. Texted actually." He fished his phone out of his pocket and flashed it in my face. The words written on it were so ludicrous, I took it out of his hand to read them for myself. Michael rarely involved himself in my life and with the fifteen-age difference between the two of us, he felt more like an uncle than a brother. His caring about me now was rich. "He's saying you and I should consummate the marriage?" I said, barely able to comprehend the archaic request.

"Your father's wishes, apparently," Gio said. "They didn't say anything to you?" His voice was so soft, one might have thought he was concerned, but I wasn't dumb enough to think that.

"My father would rather die than talk sex to me," I said. "As for my brother, well, he and I rarely speak so, this is odd. I married you for Christ's sake. What more do they want?"

"It was actually in the agreement. Didn't you read it?"

Actually, I had skimmed it. I was too shocked to find out that Gio wanted to marry me to read the damn contract clearly. What else was in there? What if? "They can't expect kids to come out of this, can they?"

"You really didn't read a damn thing, didn't you?" His annoying smirk was back, and I wanted to punch it off his face.

"I don't care. I'm not having your kids."

"The feeling's mutual," he replied. I don't know why, but hearing him say that was a stab to my heart. It made no sense. "However," he continued, "your father seems insistent on this."

"So? Just tell them we consummated the marriage. It's not like they want a blood-stained white sheet." Knowing my father's archaic sensibilities, he probably would demand one.

"I was planning on that until a new opportunity dawned me. Why not make it real? If you want my money, you have to at least show me some appreciation."

"Is this your way of humiliating me?"

He stepped forward, eliminating the small space between us. I took in a deep breath as he leaned in and kissed my neck. He placed another kiss a little further up, and another until he reached my mouth and placed a light but persistent kiss. Whatever part of me that wanted to resist slowly disappeared, and I let him delve into my mouth. His tongue danced with mine as he deepened the kiss. I stifled a moan as he assaulted my senses with just his tongue and lips. It felt like the first time all over again. As if nothing bad happened between us and we were back in Greece, enjoying each other. "Is this humiliating?" he whispered against my lips before kissing me again. The fog that was cocooning me lifted as the meaning of what he was saying registered. Somewhere within me, I found the strength to push him away.

He chuckled. "Looks like I still have the same effect on you as I did before."

"Right back at you," I said, pointing at his tented pants.

"I'm a warm-blooded man, Simona. It has nothing to do with you in particular. You could be any woman, and I would have the same reaction."

"You're a piece of shit."

"Doesn't stop you from wanting to fuck me."

I hate how he was right. With a simple kiss, he had awakened something in me I thought was dead. Not since... well, not since the last time I was with him I've ever felt like a horny little teenager simply from a kiss.

"Think of it this way. It would be the most profitable fuck you'd ever have. I doubt you got a million dollars, plus potentially more, from your other marks. You certainly didn't get that much from me."

So he still saw me as a woman who fucked men and to stole their money. He thought what happened in Greece was something I did all the time. The inaccuracy about it all was so funny I felt a laughter bubble inside me. It was partially true. But if I told him the whole, but I doubt he would believe me if I told him. He would think I was lying, and I didn't have the strength to dredge up the past. I had moved on from that part of my life and I wanted it over with. But if he wanted to think of me as some floozy who uses her body to get money out of men, then why not? Let him think about that. It would mean he would never have to be nice to me like he was in Greece. I would never have to fear falling for him, and that was good. When all of this is over, I would return to my life with my heart protected, my head held high, and some money in my pocket. He wanted a slut. I was going to give him a slut.

Mustering all the confidence I could, I took a step back and unpinned the first button on my blouse. Then the second. Gio raised an eyebrow. I unpinned the rest of the buttons, removed the blouse, and threw it on the couch. His nostrils flared. I thought he was going to make a move, but it seemed like he wanted me to remove all my clothes. So much for this not being some humiliation exercise. The skirt followed. I unzipped it and let it drop to the floor.

"Well," I said, standing with just my bra and panties. "Aren't you going to—" before I could finish, he grabbed my hand and swung me into his arms and gave me a hard kiss, blowing every thought out of my head. His hands were all over me all at once. From my boobs, which he palmed with passion, that surprised me, down to my butt, which he grabbed and used to draw my groin against his erection.

He broke the kiss and moved his lips down to my neck and to my breasts, where he kissed the top of each before snapping the bra open. I let it fall down as he took one breast into his mouth and flicked the nipple, resulting in a trail of electric shock that went from my breast to my clit. When I moaned, he bit the nipple, as if he didn't want me to derive pleasure, but I was so broken that the pain made me hotter.

I clutched him tightly with my hands, then moved them to his chest to take off his jacket and tie with little finesse. While I was busy with his clothes, he ripped off my panties. I could only undo a few of his buttons before he let go of me and turned me around and pushed me onto the couch. There was no gentleness in his touch. It differed from all the previous times we had sex.

Maybe it was because he had changed, but that could not be it. He wanted to punish me and I liked it. A masochistic part of me wanted him to be rougher.

I fell onto my knees on the couch, facing away from him, my legs splayed. My sensitive nipples and exposed clit brushed against the velvet fabric, and a moan escaped me. I heard him groan from behind. I probably looked like the slut he thought I was from his vantage point, and instead, wetness gushed out of my pussy at the thought.

The couch dipped and felt his body against my back, pushing me into the couch. I watched as his hand snake to my left breast, hold it and brush the nipple against the couch. I bit back another moan. "Fuck," I said, as he did the same to the other nipple.

"Do you like that?" he whispered in my ear.

My, "Yes," came out strained as my hips gyrated in time to his movements, brushing my clit against the couch and my butt against his erection. He removed his hands from my breasts and I almost protested in frustration, but he moved down to my pussy. "You're already wet," he whispered against my neck as he played with my clit, edging me that much closer to ecstasy. I felt him remove his pants with his other hand, followed by the sound of a condom being ripped open. He removed his hand from my clit for a short while as I heard him put on the condom. Then he was nudging my leg aside and his hand was back against my pussy before entering me with a deep thrust. My breath caught as Gio drew me up and then down onto his cock. Was it bigger than I remembered? Probably not, but it felt like it was so. Maybe because it had been a while since I had been with anyone. He thrust again, in and out. Deeper and faster. He grabbed my neck, drawing me back for a kiss that felt like it intended to hurt, but the position meant he went in that much deeper. He was rough, and it was obvious he didn't care about my pleasure, but the motion of his thrusts resulted in my nipples and clit rubbing against the couch, increasing my pleasure. In no time, I could see that cliff coming and I screamed in ecstasy just as I felt him tighten and then moan out loud.

We stayed stuck together in that position for a couple minutes as we both caught our breaths. I moaned again when he removed his cock from my still sensitive center and stood up. I turned to face him. He was smirking as he tucked his cock back into his pants like some long-held belief of his had been confirmed. I had a sneaking suspicion what that belief was. And isn't it exactly how I wanted to be viewed, anyway? So why did I feel like I had lost?

4

GIOVANNI

I hate her. I hate everything about her and the hold she has on me. A day later, I was still thinking about the explosive, impulsive sex we had. It was an act meant to teach her a lesson. Show her what she meant to me; nothing. A cum receptacle. But I did not achieve that. Quite the opposite, actually. She was with me throughout. Her cries were those of someone enjoying the act. I even made sure she was enjoying herself instead of doing what I planned to do, humiliate her.

Maybe that was it. Someone like her could not feel the humiliation. Not only that, but something else happened that's only happened with one other woman, her. I wanted her again. I thought my lust for her was over, but clearly, it wasn't. I had to wake up in the middle of the night and douse myself in a cold shower just so I wouldn't go to her room. But that only helped a little. I hardly slept.

As a result, I left the apartment earlier than usual, before she woke up and escaped her intoxicating presence. That didn't mean my mind escaped her. I was still thinking about her two hours later, after getting into the office and telling myself I was going to concentrate on nothing but work. For the next four hours, I did everything to concentrate on the present. The drab meetings I had to attend didn't help. Instead of listening to the junior executive's presentation on our fund's current risk profile, my mind kept wandering to the image of Simona's beautiful boobs bouncing up and down as I thrust into in her again and again. By the end of the day, I wanted to end the pretense, have her come over to my office and suck my dick. It would not be a task she would agree to. The hate in her eyes the last time I saw her was all the proof I need.

The funny thing is, I should be the angry one.

She had almost ruined our plans by continuing to work at that place of hers. As much as I loved Judy, she was now in bed with our enemy. Saccone wanted to place his claws into anything connected to our father. Their rival ran deep. He was probably using Judy and if Saccone knew my wife worked for her, he would have used that as leverage against me and against the family. Hell, he might have kidnapped Simona while she was at work and would have had a piece to use against us. And how would that have looked to my brothers? It wouldn't be the first time I would have sabotaged the business via Simona.

My phone chimed, taking me out of my thoughts. My eyes refocused on the reports on my laptop screen. The same reports I had opened this morning. I might as well admit nothing was getting done today. I glanced at the phone and scowled. "Is it done?" The message was from Simona's brother. He had been pestering me since the wedding. Her family wanted us to stay in Tuscany for a week, probably to ensure Simona and I had consummated the wedding. However, Saccone's intimidation tactic of crashing the wedding made us leave early.

Did the Vannuccis think I was going to annul the marriage? As if my brothers would let me. I picked up the phone and typed, "It's done."

Three dots scrolled for a few seconds, then a message popped up. "How do I know?" I squashed the urge to roll my eyes and punched in my reply to him. "Do you want me to send you a picture of the sheets? Maybe the sheets themselves? Wanna test them for DNA?" I dropped the phone on the table in anger. I was getting annoyed with him. What happened between me and Simona should stay between us, no matter what her family thought. The phone chimed again. "Lol." The first text read. Followed by, "I hate this as much as you do. Do you think I want to know whether my sister has had sex? Anyway, I will forward the message." At least he felt as squeamish as any brother would. I wondered if Simona's old-fashioned father knew about her exploits? That she's a well-known party girl and socialite, or did he demand such archaic terms because he knew what kind of daughter he had?

"Mr. Morelli." A voice from the intercom boomed. I clicked the answer button. "Giovanni. I told you before," I said to my assistant. My assistant, however, was new and still learning the ropes and hearing her referring to me in such a formal manner invoked the aura of a Don. The last thing I wanted people from the legal side of the business to think of me as. Being less formal with them meant they were less likely to see me as an unapproachable king and come to me with problems quicker. It was the opposite when it came to the underground. You wanted the men to fear you or they would run rug shod all over you.

"Right, of course," she said. "Sorry, Mr. — I mean Giovanni. There's a man here saying he wants to see you urgently, but he didn't have an appointment…"

"Who is he?"

"A Mr. Lewis." "William Lewis?" Why would my detective want a meeting with me? My heart skipped a beat. I had sent him on a specific assignment a few weeks ago. He could not have dug up information already. "Send him in," I said.

The huge bulking man marched in. As a former police detective, he had a seriousness designed to put fear into suspects, something he seemed to have never let go. "Lewis," I said to him, "You're already done with your investigation?"

He settled down into a chair opposite my desk and placed a notepad he was holding on it. His brown hair flopped to his forehead as he did so, making this veteran detective look oddly boyish. "I hope I'm not disturbing or anything," he said, a little more serious than usual, but then again, he was always serious. "But I thought you'd want to know what I found out immediately."

"You're freaking me out a little. What is she up to?"

"That's the thing," he said. Lewis took out his phone and continued talking as he tapped and swiped on it. "I was in the middle of looking into her past. So far I haven't found anything that we didn't know yet. But—and I swear I wasn't following her—I saw her in a particular part of the town. I didn't expect to see her, if you know what I mean. So, I followed her and guess who I saw her with." He handed me his phone.

When I saw the image on display, I felt like flinging the phone to the wall. Why she thought going there was a good idea flummoxed me. She was goading me. It was the only plausible explanation. She was part of our world. She should know better. "This was today?" I asked, my hand trembling as I barely reined in the anger. Lewis nodded. "I thought you should know," he added.

I flipped to the next image and then the next. Each one more damning that the last. They were all images of my wife Simona, seemingly comfy with her ex-boyfriend, or current boyfriend, for all I know. While the images didn't show the two kissing or anything more, they showed enough proof of intimacy. The way she looked into his eyes. She has never looked at me like that.

"So, they're still together," I said to more to myself, but Lewis responded, "I'm not sure. I could look into it. Come back with more concrete proof if you like." I gave him his phone back and back in his pocket. He said, "It might mean nothing. They could be friends. It might be a business meeting or something."

I could tell that Lewis was trying to comfort me in his own way, but those pictures, innocent as they were, showed there was something still going on between them. It was definitely not a business meeting. "I doubt it," I said, trying not to sound as bitter as I felt.

"Do you want me to look into it?" Lewis said.

I nodded. "She shouldn't be seeing him, regardless. He's part of the Bianchis and she was in their territory. We have an uneasy truce with the Bianchi family, but that doesn't mean they're allies." And besides, I didn't want to make an enemy out of them while our family was already at war with another family. And where were her bodyguards? They were nowhere in the images, even though I had assigned them to her this morning. I strictly told them not to let her go to the off-limits areas of the city. God, she was a constant headache.

If she wasn't running a scheme, then I didn't

understand what she wanted with him. She was the wife of one of the richest and influential men in the city. She had everything she desired. I even gave her money to start her own business. What else would she want? Was it the thrill or was it to get back at me?

I dismissed Lewis and made a mental note to raise his salary. He was the only former cop I had on my payroll, but he was more loyal than any of my men. Even the bodyguards I had assigned to Simona weren't so loyal. They should have called me when they realized where she was taking them. I made a call to one of them. Luckily for him, he answered on the third ring. "Where are you?" I asked.

"Uh, good day Mr. Morelli. Your wife is currently looking at office space."

"Is that where you are?"

Johnny cleared his throat. I could not see it, but I could tell he was adjusting his collar. "Of course, Mr. Morelli. Where would we be?" In the background, I heard Simona say, "Is that Giovanni, Johnny?" At least they were together. "And where were you in the afternoon?" I heard him gulp, followed by a pregnant pause. "Lost your tongue there, Johnny?"

"Not at all sir," he said, "It's just that when Simona—"

"First name basis? With my wife?" The trio had only spent hours together, and they were talking to each other as if they were long-time friends. That feeling of hurling the phone to the wall came back again, and I had to clamp it down.

"I'm sorry. I mean, Mrs. Morelli asked to be taken to that borough. We told her it was a no-go territory, but she insisted and since the Bianchis aren't—" Johnny's voice trailed off and another came onto the line.

"Are you stalking me?" Simona's sultry voice came out from the other end. My body instantly responded as my cock hardened just from hearing her and remembering what we did last night. I hated the effect she had on me.

I got up from my seat and went to the window where I gazed at the view of the city made into a beautiful golden skyline as the sun set. "Sounds like you're on a first name basis with my men already. What made them obey you instead of me, I wonder. Did you give them one of your glorious blow jobs?" I winced as soon as the words came out. They were not only below the belt, but worse, they made me sound like a jealous husband. Johnny and Mickey were my most trusted bodyguards. I had assigned them to Simona because I knew she would be safe with them and the two would rather die than act untoward to her.

"Fuck off, Gio. Honestly," she spat.

"Is that what you were doing with your old boyfriend? Or should I say current?"

"Oh my god, you're stalking me. You creep! Having two of your men with me at all times is not enough, apparently. You added a third tail."

I was the one who should yell, not her. She was the one caught cheating. "I didn't have to. You were so public with your indiscretions people saw you."

"Indiscretions? Do you even hear yourself? I can't visit an old friend now!"

I was about to mouth off that Leonardo wasn't just an old friend to her and scream that he was her ex until I stopped myself. Best for her to not know what I knew. It could be information I could use later.

"Is that what he is? Just a friend?"

"Yes! And if I knew that his part of town was off limits and so dangerous that I shouldn't even visit," she dragged the phrase 'off limits,' "I wouldn't have gone."

"Yeah, don't go. And stop seeing Leonardo."

"Why?"

"If you continue to do so, Johnny and Mickey can say bye to their time on earth."

"What—"

I ended the call there for emphasis. I wasn't going to kill her bodyguards, of course. They have been with me longer than I knew Simona. Johnny and Mickey probably thought it prudent to do as she said. It was all Simona's fault. She was the one testing my patience, and eventually, she was going to learn the consequences of toying around with me.

5

SIMONA

He came back home angry. I was worried he would do something when he entered, but he instead marched past me and went upstairs. I fucked up and worse, I might jeopardize two lives. The threat he had laid on me the last time we spoke on the phone left a chill down my spine. Sure, I cajoled Johnny and Mickey into taking me to visit Leonardo. When they learned the part of town I wanted to go to; they were adamant about not taking me there, but I told them it would only be a few minutes, and it was. All I wanted to do was tell Leonardo I was in town and see how he was doing. He was a friend of mine, after all.

How Gio found out was the most peculiar part. He must have had a third person following me. There's no way the bodyguards would have said anything to me. Not with the way they were apprehensive during my visit. Mickey was grumbling throughout the ride and only felt a little better when I offered them to go to lunch with me afterward. They were nice guys, and did not deserve whatever wrath Gio had planned for them.

"You have to understand that it was me who persuaded them to take me there," I said as soon as he came downstairs and into the living room. "If I had known it was that serious, I wouldn't have forced them."

"I didn't know a meeting with your boyfriend was important enough to risk a shaky truce. Surprised you were still horny after last night. Or do you still want more?"

"He's not my boyfriend."

"I don't care. Stay away from him."

"Fine. But I need to know why. You can't just tell me not to do anything or not to go anywhere."

"Simona." He massaged his forehead, a

subconscious sign that he was annoyed with me. "It's for your own good."

"You took my job away, because it was for my own good. Now you've taken my liberty to move around in the city, which, according to you, is for my own good. But I'm sorry, this sounds like obsessive-possessive behavior to me." He growled. I wasn't going to be threatened. I folded my arms in defiance. He could growl all day for all I care, but he wasn't going to scare me. The only people I worried about were Johnny and Mickey, who I had accidentally roped into this feud.

Instead of responding, he turned his attention away from me and took out his phone from his pocket, glanced at it and put it back. "You and I should be leaving. We have an event to attend."

"Not until you answer me."

"Will you agree if I agree to tell you on the way?"

"And what if I don't want to go?"

"You won't get your answer. Simple as that."

"And Johnny and Mickey?"

"You seem to care a lot about those two men." Did I detect jealousy? No. His curt reply probably had to do with him being angry at me than anything else. Besides, he seemed to give them the same attention he gave his furniture.

"I don't want anything to happen to them

because of what I did."

"I promise no harm will come to them. But they're going to have to learn a lesson."

Visions of Giovanni's men whipping Johnny and Mickey, pulling their nails with pincers and electrocuting their balls, came to mind. He didn't seem like he could be that ruthless, but his family was well known to be capable of harsh violence toward people they deemed enemies. "You're not going to torture them, are you?"

Gio chuckled. "I meant docking their pay. God, you must think I'm some ruthless maniac."

"Well, aren't you?"

Gio stalked over to me until there was little space between us. It felt difficult to breathe when he was this close. My gaze went to his lips, remembering the way they had played against mine yesterday. I had struggled the entire day to get those erotic thoughts out of my mind, but having him this close made it impossible. They flooded in. His grip on my waist. The way he had played my body like fiddle and gave me an orgasm that I hadn't gotten from anyone else but me in a long time. Coupled with the eroticism, however, was the edge to him. That danger that effortlessly emanated from his being.

If I was as bad as you think, you wouldn't be disobeying me. If anyone is the villain here, it's you."

"Me?"

"Some would consider stealing money from people as evil."

Ah. That. Should I tell him the truth? I wanted to tell him. I wanted him to see me in a good light. Maybe if he knew the truth, he wouldn't treat me as terrible as he did, but I stopped myself just in time. He was likely to remain as hateful and become even more vengeful, not just to me, but to someone else I love, and I couldn't let that happen. Being the only person to receive his wrath was better than the alternative. "I'm sorry, I stole your money, but really? It was a long time ago, and I am sure a man as proficient in the arts of finance as you has since made it back many times over."

"It's not just about that and you know it."

"What else could it be?" I asked. I doubt he was bothered by the lies I had told him all those years ago about coming back with him to New York and becoming his girlfriend. It's not as if he didn't lie. He had told me he wanted to continue our relationship beyond our Greek vacation, but I doubt he wanted someone like me, a party slut, as he had called me, as a girlfriend. The words hurt then, and they still do now, but that's how I had deliberately painted myself as.

He shook his head as if dismissing some thought that came to mind, and suddenly his mood shifted and he changed the topic. "We need to get ready."

I wanted to get into it with him more. I wanted to know what this other thing could be, but I let him change the subject. "Where are we going?"

"A gallery opening."

"One of your money laundering schemes?"

"We need to be seen out together at a few locations if we want people to think this as a genuine relationship."

"Why would anyone care?"

"Wanna know? I'll tell you on the way." He checked his phone again and then glanced back at me with eyes clouded with passion. "Or maybe you want us to spend tonight the same way we spent last night." His eyes lowered to my chest. "I have a hankering to see them bounce up and down as I fuck you against the window."

I instinctively clutched my chest. "I'll get ready," I said and made my way to my bedroom. How was he able to turn it on and off like that, leaving me with a jumble of emotions? I ran out, not because I want to go to this gallery opening, but because the thought of getting fucked against his wall to ceiling windows had me flushing red. It was embarrassing to go from being angry at him to wanting to fuck him in a matter of seconds.

I quickly searched for something that would look good at a gallery opening, added some jewelry, and made my way back downstairs. Gio was waiting for me and he too had changed as well. The gray pants and light-blue shirt paired with a dark navy blazer made him exude the energy of a modern-day roman god. My stomach fluttered the moment I laid eyes on him. This man is my husband, I thought.

Gio's gaze scanned me up and down as I descended the staircase. "Will I do?" I asked.

"You look fine." I rolled my eyes. It's not like I was expecting platitudes. I didn't need him to tell me that my black silk jumpsuit was cute, but 'fine' was a bit dismissive. He could act like he wasn't affected by me, but I was sure I saw his nostrils flair when his gaze landed on my dipping neckline.

He led me out of the apartment and when we got to the car, I was glad to see Mickey holding the passenger door open and Johnny in the driver's seat. I mouthed a sorry at Mickey as I got in and got a glare from Gio.

Once the car was on the road, I turned to Gio and said, "I held up my end of the bargain. Now you." For a moment, I thought he wasn't going to say anything. He seemed occupied with typing something on his phone, but he eventually flipped it down on his lap. "The Morelli family is currently at war with the Saccones, that part I'm sure you knew," he said.

I shook my head.

"No?" He frowned. "Your father never told you anything?"

"I stay out of that part of his business. All I knew is you were at war with some other rival family."

"You're a mafia princess. The least you should do is know what your family is up to. At the very least, for your own protection."

"My father... never mind."

"Your father is traditional and considers it 'men's' business?"

"Something like that."

"The insistence on consummation tipped me to it." I don't know if it was the low glow of the streetlights streaming in the car, but I was sure his features had turned soft and there seemed to be sympathy in his eyes. Even his voice sounded gentle. However, he bounced back to business mode and continued with the explanation. "We've been in a cold war with the Saccone family and it's only heated recently. And since Saccone's foothold is Vegas, same as ours, it has only made things tense. My brothers who operate there have been dealing with the brunt of the war. Dante was almost killed in an ambush. It happened in Brazil, but the men did it on Saccone's orders. "

Holy fuck. I froze in my seat. Everything seemed to shrink down to the confines of the car as I listened to what he was saying. I knew something was going on with the Morellis and their enemies. I know what my husband does. But somehow, I never thought it was would be this serious. My voice came out small and strained. "Is he okay?"

"It happened before the wedding," he said.

All Gio's brothers were there, and they all seemed fine. The entire ceremony was a whirlwind, but I specifically remember Dante being caring and sweet towards me. He had even asked me if I was sure if I wanted to get married and that the Morellis would not mind if I called off the wedding.

"One of his men was badly injured though, so blood was spilled. Which is where you come in."

"Marrying me guarantees the support of my family?"

Gio nodded.

"What about the Bianchis? Are they your enemy too?"

"The Bianchis are staying out of it. But giving them a reason to, say, ransom the wife of one of the Morelli brothers to Saccone, would make them our enemy. That's why I don't want you in their territory. They could leave you alone, they could ransom you back to us. But if they get other ideas…"

"I get it. You don't want me getting in the middle of your war and causing all sorts of chaos."

"Leonardo, being a Bianchi, is also why I don't want you to see him, no matter the nature of your relationship." I wanted to tell him again that nothing was going on between me and Leo, but I doubt he would believe me. My visit was an innocent one. I had asked Leo to join me in my new business and he had declined. The whole truce/war thing was probably why.

"What about Judy? Why did you stop me working at her magazine?"

"Saccone is using Judy's business as a money laundering scheme. She used to come to us when she needed money, and I would have given her a loan on good terms. I don't know why she went to Saccone. Regardless. If you were still working there and Saccone found out…"

He would have kidnapped me and used me as a bargaining chip. Or worse, kill me and mail my head to Giovanni. For the first time, it settled on me how serious all of this was. Gio didn't seem worried at all, but I was beginning to worry for him. "Are you safe? This sounds—"

"New York is where we deal with the legal end of the business. He's not going to shoot me down while I'm taking a stroll in the park, but one can't be too careful. Do you get now why I want you to stay safe?"

"Why didn't you tell me all of this before?"

"Because I don't trust you. I only told you now, because you refuse to behave. It's better you know than have you acting like a headless chicken."

"I don't know, maybe, I wouldn't be acting like a headless chicken if I knew you were in the middle of a war where I could die. What's your beef with Saccone, anyway?"

"We have no beef with him. He had beef with our father however. Old shit that only a few know. He saw a weakness in our business when our father died and capitalized. That's it. Just business. He thinks we are so weak he was audacious enough to gate crush our wedding."

"What the fuck! He was at our wedding? When?" I scanned my brain for an unfamiliar face at the wedding reception, but everyone there was someone I knew or someone I knew to be related to the Morellis. It was a small affair.

"He came with his entourage while you were inside the villa and caused a scene before leaving. He was just flexing his muscles." There was a time before the reception started when Giovanni told me to stay inside while they were setting up the marquee. I didn't think much of it back then and went to the kitchen to thank the caterers for baking a wedding cake in such a short time. I had stayed longer than I intended because the caterer was talkative and kept asking me to taste the food to see if I liked it. Looking back, I felt like a dumb little woman for not knowing something major like that had gone down.

"Should we be going out if things are that heated?"

"Feeling a little self-preservation? Don't worry? He won't strike at a public event. Besides, his base is not in New York. If he tries anything here, he will provoke other New York families. But like I said—"

"You can't be too careful," I finished for him.

I was in a daze for the rest of the ride. Knowing that I was a pawn to be played whichever way by multiple mafia crime families did not put me at ease. Gio was confident going to the gallery opening was safe, but what if he was wrong? What if one of his enemies was careless enough that they would try to kill us there? How could he live such a life and be so calm?

"Simona?" I turned to my left to see the car door was open and Giovanni standing outside with his hand stretched out. I was so deep in my thoughts I didn't notice the car coming to a stop, Gio getting out and the door being opened. I tried to ignore my overwhelming anxiety and took his hand.

The gallery was in one of the most fashionable areas of the city, but that still didn't stop thoughts of gunmen coming out of the night and railing bullets into my chest.

"Are you sure we'll be safe?" I asked.

Gio seemed bemused with my statement and I expected a snarky retort, but he said, "Like I said before, no one would dare attack us at such an event." He caressed my hand softly. "Besides, my men would never let that happen." Right. Of course. I was being overly worried. It's just that I had no idea how in danger I was until now. I clamped down on my worry and let him lead me inside. It was going to be fine. Everything was going to be fine.

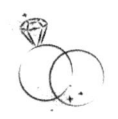

We were handed glasses of champagne and

pamphlets as we entered and welcomed by the owner, a middle-aged man in a white suit who greeted Giovanni with sweet familiarity. "A friend of yours?" I asked after the owner was gone and we started making our way through the gallery. Gio nodded.

"Another investment?" I asked as we stopped at the first painting.

He raised his eyebrows, clearly understanding what I meant by investment. "I told you. I only deal with the legal side of the business and no, this is not one of my *legal* investments," he said.

"Interesting. So you're like the money man in your family? You never told me the hierarchy."

He narrowed his eyes. "Why? Is there someone who wants the information?"

"Oh, god. I was just asking out of interest. Making small talk with my husband. That sort of thing."

He sighed, and I felt his hand, which had gone to my waist, tighten and then soften. "If there's a hierarchy, Dante is the head. Followed by me and then the twins, Rico and Nico."

"See," I said, taking a swig of the champagne. "That wasn't so hard."

We continued with the tour. The pieces were grouped by artist and most of the contemporary ones had the artist standing by, ready to explain their work. There were people buying the art, as some pieces had stickers marked sold below. Most of the art was good. The gallery owner seemed to have a good eye, but Gio, for someone who had dragged me here, didn't seem that interested in what was on display. He was walking a little too fast to appreciate the art.

"You know, if we walk a little faster, we will be done touring in a couple of minutes," I said. He mumbled something I didn't catch and shuffled me forward. His rushed attitude hit something in me. Instead of I stopped. "I don't know about you, but I would rather savor the art, you know, before moving on."

"Really? You want to savor this?"

It's just so happened that we had stopped in the photography section, the least inspired section of the gallery if I were to put it nicely. "I mean, not this piece in particular." It was probably the worst piece in the gallery. A black-and-white photograph of a mouse that looked like a filter had been added to it instead of being taken by black and white film. I knew little about art, but even I could tell it was not worth even hanging in a cheap motel. "This piece is making me reconsider your friend's eye for art," I said.

"That's because the benefactor of this fine place has a new wife who thinks she's an artist. And for the owner to get funding, he had to agree to showcasing this." His last words were laced with derision. Not that it wasn't deserved. The 'artist', if I could call her that, was terrible. Most of the work was out of focus, too simplistic or just downright bad.

"Simona?"

I turned to the source of the familiar voice and tone. Someone I hadn't seen in a long time was standing behind us. "Kara?"

She immediately rushed towards me and enveloped me in a hug. When she let me go, she said, "Where have you been hiding!"

"Around." I was feeling self-conscious suddenly. Kara and I used to go clubbing together, back when I had too much time on my hands and wanted to get away from my mother. We were close at one point. If Kara started chatting—and she loved to chat—about all those times we got drunk together, Giovanni's already low opinion of me would go down to below zero.

"Who would have thought that I would see you here? You've always hated this scene."

"I could say the same about you," I said, wondering what she was doing here. She laughed. "I'm a different woman nowadays." She took her gaze off me and onto Gio as if noticing him for the first time. "And who is this you're with?"

I cleared my throat. "Kara, Giovanni. My...husband. Giovanni, Kara, an old friend of mine."

"Husband?" her eyes widened. "My god, Sim, you bagged a handsome one, didn't you?" She extended a hand to Gio. "Nice to meet you, Giovanni," she said.

"Same here," Gio replied, taking her hand. It didn't sound like he was pleased at all, but Kara seemed not to notice. She continued talking. "My teddy bear is around here somewhere as well." Her gaze darted around the gallery. "There he is." Kara waved over a thin man with white hair peppered with black streaks, who immediately came over to us. She pulled him close and said, "Ted, look who I found." The man, who seemed half drunk, already glanced at me without recognition, then at Gio, and his eyes brightened. "Ah, Giovanni Morelli!" he extended his hand towards him. "Didn't know art was your thing." Gio shook his hand and replied, "I'm here to support a friend. Kevin, the owner."

"I didn't know you and Morelli were friends. I could've gotten a good bargain on our last real estate deal," Ted said.

Meanwhile, Kara rolled her eyes and gently nudged Ted in the ribs. "I didn't mean him. I meant his wife, Simona?" Ted's face was blank.

"You know, my friend? The one I told you about…" When nothing registered on Ted's face, she gave up and said, "You know what, never mind." She turned her attention to me instead. "So, Sim. What do you think?"

The topics had moved so fast in such a short time; I was unsure what she was talking about. Seeing my expression, she turned to the art on the wall. "I saw you looking at the Sad mouse piece."

"Uh…" I looked down at the name below the works. Kara Sullivan, it read. Oh, god. The horrible photographs were hers. I didn't notice at first glance that this was hers. I knew her as Kara Brown. Sullivan was probably her husband's surname. I looked at Ted and Kara. Ted must be the benefactor Gio was talking about. I scrambled for something that was truthful, but not hurtful. I couldn't come up with any. "Are they yours?" I asked. Kara nodded with the giddiness of an excited child.

"My wife has quite the talent, doesn't she?"

Gio choked on his drink. I could tell he wanted to burst out laughing.

"You never told me you were into photography before," I said.

"I didn't know I had it in me. I mean, you inspired me with your whole 'I want to leave all this partying thing and start my store' spiel. You said the day you left our apartment." Kara turned to Gio. "Did you know she was the biggest club hopper in town? She could get you into any club. I don't know how she did it, had all the men in the palm of her hand. I mean, she could party hard when she wanted to and then one day she stopped." My cheeks were reddening, and I couldn't stop Kara from talking. "She wanted to try something different, she said."

"And I went for it," I said before she could embarrass me further.

"You must have your fashion line or something. How is it going?"

I couldn't lie. I was sure Gio would call me out. And when I glanced at him, he did not look like an ally. He was enjoying me squirming. "I got off that before I even started. Turns out I'm not as good a designer as I thought I was." It was the truth. After my partying stint, I applied to fashion houses, and they practically laughed my designs out of the room. That was when I went to Judy's magazine and worked as a stylist. At least that I could do.

Kara's face fell. "Oh. I would have thought you'd be like Donatella by now." She quickly moved on by talking about herself. "Anyway, one day, I started taking fewer pictures of myself and more of other things and posting it on social media. People liked it. And then Teddy Bear bought me like a film camera and I just went on from there."

"Art comes naturally to some, I guess," Ted said.

"That's true," Gio said. "You either have it or you don't." Ted and Kara did not detect his sarcastic tone, but I did. He didn't need to have it spelled out for him to get that I was rejected from fashion design.

"Does that mean you like it?" Kara said, clasping her hands under her chin.

"Simona was the one who was interested. Weren't you Sim?"

I glared at him. "It stopped me in my tracks," I said to Kara. What else could I say without sounding jealous?

"Do you want to buy it?" Kara asked.

"Uh… what?"

"It's not even that expensive since I'm a new artist and all. None of my works are above five thousand." Five thousand! How did any of this shit get anywhere near the five thousand range?

"I don't think—" I was thinking of a way to wiggle out of buying gently, but she railroaded me. "This will cost two thousand. What do you think?" Fuck. How was I going to get out of this?

It's not like I had that much money to spend on a photo. Technically I did, but I wasn't going to spend it on a shitty photograph made by my not so friendly friend from years past. "Kara, I don't think—"

Gio cut into my stumbling apology. "It would look great in your new store," Gio said. I had to avoid stomping on his foot. The store was still at the ideas stage, barely concrete, but the thought of this ugly ass 'artwork' going in it coiled my stomach. I scrambled to think of something to counter Gio without shitting on Kara, but my hesitation and, "Uh…" only made Kara's eyes widen positively. "I guess," I said.

Kara leaped with excitement. "My first sale! I can't believe it! I'll be right back. I need to put your name down and look for that sold thingy." She sped off and Ted followed her, after thanking me again.

When they were safely out of earshot, Gio started laughing. "You seem to be enjoying this," I said.

"I just love seeing your gold digger friend fleecing money out of you. It feels like karma."

Of course, he thought so. He was enjoying my humiliation. Part of me couldn't help but wonder if he brought me here, knowing Kara would be here, and that we knew each other from before.

The gallery no longer held the same excitement as before. The room felt too full of people, too stuffy and the wine too warm. I downed the rest of the champagne and handed the empty glass to a passing waiter. "Now that my spanking is complete, can we leave now?"

"Not yet."

"You have another humiliation scene set up?"

"Not everything is about you," Gio scoffed.

We turned a corner and reached what I assumed to be a restricted section of the gallery, if the guard at the entrance was anything to go by. Giovanni showed the man a card and he let us through. The area had an interesting selection of art, mostly paintings. It was definitely the more eclectic part of the gallery. Unlike the earlier sections, this one did not have artists standing next to their art. I stopped to look at the pieces. One was a small Picasso, the size of a pocketbook. The one next to it looked like a Warhol. They were fewer patrons here, but one could tell most were here not to look, but to do business. One man in particular examined a Basquiat with a magnifying glass as if examining its authenticity.

While strolling, I got distracted by all the priceless art around me, and almost bumped into Gio when he halted. Finally, something had captured his interest. It was an art piece of an abstract woman painted in black, crying into a river that turned into a sea of gold with specks of black. It was a striking piece.

Even though Giovanni hadn't been much of a talker ever since we arrived. He fell deeper into silence as he stared at the painting. "Found what you were looking for?" I said, looking for a way to fill the uncomfortable silence. There was something about the painting that was mocking me. As if it was saying something that I should understand, but was failing to.

"Yes." His voice was gruff. I couldn't see his face. He was standing in front of me, but I could not deny the heavy emotion in his voice.

"Sounds like you find it moving."

"How can I not?" he turned to face me. If he had been feeling anything soft, it was all gone. Rage and disgust were what I saw on his face when he said, "I had to sell it because of your stealing."

I almost wanted to roll my eyes. He was being a little dramatic. A man like him had more than enough money that I doubt he felt it the way he seemed to claim. The dude was vacationing in Greece on a yacht when we met. "Do you want a sorry? Sorry. Who's the artist anyway, so I can tell them how affected you are by their art?" That last sentence. I don't know what made me utter it, but I wanted to hurt him the same way he was hurting me. However, his response was the last thing I expected to hear and made instantly regret my statement.

"My mother."

6

GIOVANNI

The painting was just as I remembered. Whoever had it before had maintained it properly. The gold of the water, whilst a little brown than I recalled, still had a shimmering tone to it that contrasted the black paint of the woman. Just looking at it brought back a wash of memories I thought were long gone. Memories of her painting this exact piece. She would let me into her studio, a privilege only I ever gotten, and let me watch her work. Giving this up was hard.

When Kevin told me he found the painting, I

thought I was going to come in here, buy it back and walk out. Overwhelming emotions were the last thing I expected. Maybe it was because of the person I came with. Simona was the reason I had to sell it. And here she was, standing next to me, mocking me.

"I'm sorry," she said. It sounded sincere, but I would be a fool to trust a professional liar like her.

"No need for the apology, Simona. I know you don't care." I turned back to the painting. There was no price on it, but if Kevin put it on display, he probably thought it was going to fetch a higher price from other buyers. There were art collectors in here and most of them probably did not recognize it because it's a different style than the one she's known for. But if one of them looked closer... Well, that's not going to happen. I signaled to Mickey, who had been following us discreetly throughout and told him to make sure no one ever comes near the painting except us. His intimidating body would probably be enough to scare most of these artsy folks.

"When we took your money..."

"You're still talking," I said without looking at her. I thought it would be enough to dismiss her. I was doing everything I could to show her how cold I was, even though a part of me was feeling the exact opposite.

"Come on, Gio. Can I at least explain myself?"

Without wanting to, without thinking, I turned to face her again as if compelled by a mystical force. She had a mask of sincerity again. I ignored it. I might fall for it if I wasn't careful and turned my gaze away from her face, only for it to land onto her enticing cleavage. Her jumpsuit was form-fitting and elegant. It dipped low at the chest, making her breasts appear like two round apples begging to be licked. An idea popped into my head of dragging her away from her into an empty room I saw earlier and fucking her senseless. Maybe that was the solution. Fuck her until I no longer felt like this, because right now, she was making me feel nothing but conflicting emotions, and I hated it. Order and sense was what my life was about and she was bringing in chaos and destruction.

"You had a yacht. I didn't think you'd miss a million dollars."

"Yeah, you don't think, do you? It wasn't the one million dollars that set me back. It was the chain of dominos you started. Because of your actions, I ended up losing a lot more money than what you stole. But that's the problem with people like you. You don't think about anyone beyond yourself."

Thing is, she didn't steal my money, but a client's money just when we were illiquid. The client ended up telling everyone in his circle that my hedge fund was a Ponzi scheme and his circle told people in their circles. On and on it went, resulting in the company losing money and clients. Then it all coincided with a stock market crash, which made the loss so much larger that the company almost went into bankruptcy. It's funny when you think about it. Many have tried to take down the Morelli family and failed. The only person who came close was a scamming little party girl.

"What did you do with the money, anyway?" She looked away and did not respond. My bet was shoes and clothes. She seemed to love wearing all the best things. What else could she have spent it on?

"What do you think? Am I a genius or not?" I turned my gaze away from Simona to Kevin, who was smiling as he came over to us. Mickey stopped him in his tracks and looked at me for assent. I nodded once and he let Kevin go. "Your boy is tough, guarding you against me, in my gallery. Or," he squinted his left eye as he leaned forward, "you don't want people to know a Coretti is in the gallery." Beside me, Simona choked. "Maria Coretti?" I heard her whisper.

"Including your brand-new wife?" Kevin said in mock disapproval. "I gotta say, that's cold."

"How much is it?" Because of how famous she was before she died and because she had few paintings, her work was often expensive. Kevin, like the money grubber I knew him to be, mentioned a sum so big that Simona let out a strangled gasp.

"Her work has only gone up in value as the years pass. Who knows, I might sell it to you at a bargain. I could open it up to auction."

He really was trying to fleece me. That was the problem of being the suit-wearing one in the family. Everyone assumed you were straight and forgot that you came from a line of killers. I shifted my weight onto one foot and pretended to think. "An auction. That sounds like a great idea. You could do one of those. But then if you choose that road, it won't be just Mickey over there I would come with. Maybe, let's say hypothetically, I could come with a few more mickeys and have them light this place up before the auction. We would take the good pieces, of course. Your little Picasso and Basquiat will come with us for safekeeping."

Kevin's eyes widened.

"But we don't have to do all that. Unlike my brothers, I'm a man of business. And if I'm offered a reasonable price, I respond reasonably."

Kevin gulped. I could see sweat running down his neck and I was sure he was close to soiling himself. A smile that did not reach his eyes spread over his face. "You know me, I like to test waters. That offer was just a little tester. The actual price is…" His new price was a third of his original price. Much less than I sold it for and much less than he probably bought it for.

"Now that's reasonable," I said.

Kevin almost bowed as he shook my hand. He then said something about taking down the painting and packaging it properly before leaving. Beside me, I heard Simona draw in a deep breath. I rarely used my powers of persuasion, but Kevin had been pushing it.

"You don't mess around," she said after he was gone.

"No. I don't."

Exhilaration rushed through me. It had been a long time since I've felt like flexing my muscles and doing so just now made me feel like a king. A feeling I've never had before. Maybe it was Kevin and my slight resentment towards his trying to stiff me out of my mother's painting. Or maybe it was something else. I glanced at Simona. Maybe it was her presence and a primal need to show her strength. Some primitive feeling inside me I was sure was long since purged.

There was something about her that brought the worst parts in me. I was not like my younger brothers, Rico and Nico, who acted feral and violent whenever they were threatened. Nor was I like my older brother Dante, who, while not as feral, was just as ruthless. I saw myself as different from them, more sophisticated, but that suaveness ends up being a flimsy cover whenever she was around. She was destabilizing my formerly solid ground. I had to do something about it or otherwise my dark nature would take over.

Resolved, I took hold of Simona's hand, gave Mickey my card, ordering him to finish the purchase and led Simona out of the gallery. I ignored everyone and everything until we reached the car. I ordered Johnny to get out as I opened the backseat door and all but dragged Simona inside.

"What—"

I did something I wanted to do ever since I saw her going down the steps wearing that sexy jumpsuit. I placed my lips on hers and kissed her.

7

SIMONA

What the fuck. One moment he was making fun of me, the next he was threatening a gallery owner, and now we were in the back of his car making out like teenagers. No doubt giving the valets a show. His lips were on mine the instant he closed the door behind him. And I, like a horny teen, accepted his kisses without question. They were heady and addictive. I succumbed to his embrace, forgetting everything around me, as he always made me do. I forgot the barbs he was throwing at me earlier. I forgot his meanness. I forgot my earlier resolve to not be under his spell any more. Everything evaporated, and all was left was him and I.

As his lips dropped tiny kisses down my neck, nibbling and licking my skin, my hands were on his chest, exploring his tight body. I could never get over how strong he felt under my touch. I wanted to touch him all over, in particular there. My hands went down his chest, to his groin, and grasped his cock over his pants. He was harder than I expected. He moaned when I scrapped my nails against him. Somewhere deep inside me, I felt a sense of elation that he was hard for me and possibly had been hard for me for a while. It was pathetic to be this excited with something so basic as lust, but Giovanni, wanting you, tend to reduce a woman's brain to mush. He could hate me, but his body could never resist me. There was a certain power there that I didn't know what to do with. It was intoxicating.

Suddenly, he shifted our positions so that he ended up sitting on the seat and me on top of him. My jumpsuit felt too tight and too constricting. I wanted the whole thing off. He dragged me up against him and felt his hard length directly aligned with my center. I wanted this barrier of fabric between us gone. But Gio didn't seem like he was in a hurry. Sometime between dragging me into his car and placing me on top of him, he had slowed down and seemed to have regained his usual control. His eyes could not hide the passion he was feeling. Even with the little light we had, I could tell that his eyes were cloudy and intensely focused on me.

His hands went to the back of my suit and unzipped it. It fell to my thighs, and I kicked the rest of it off. He went to my naked thighs next and gripped them before grinding me against his crotch. It should not have felt as good as it did, but I was so worked up it felt close to the real thing. The grinding provided some relief to the fire that was burning at my center, but it wasn't enough. I wanted more. I wanted him inside me. My hands started traveling down, but he quickly put them back to his shoulders where they were and grounded me harder against him. My underwear was soaked and probably messing his pants. I closed my eyes to reach a peak that seemed almost within reach, but just out of grasp.

"Back at me," he said, tilting my chin so I could look at him. His gaze was arresting. I could not look away. "Please," I moaned and leaned downward to brush my lips against his. His tongue darted against mine. It inflamed the fire already burning inside me. How he could ignite such desire within me, I could never tell. I always thought of myself as someone with a low sex drive until he came along. With him, I was the exact opposite. It was as if he hacked my system and initiated the nymphomaniac program. With him, I became a different person.

"Please," I moaned again against his lips. "I need your cock," I said.

And just as suddenly as he dragged me out of the gallery earlier, he removed me off him as if I was a hot potato. Still delirious from his hands and mouth, I asked, "What's the problem?"

"Nothing. I was testing something, and I got the result I wanted."

"What?" My voice was drowsy with arousal, but the fog was quickly clearing.

"Put your clothes on soon before the men come back." I looked around at my surroundings, belatedly realizing where we were and what we were close to doing. I rushed to put my jumpsuit back on, aware that he still had his clothes on while I was practically naked.

He wrapped on the door the second I was done, and the two bodyguards entered the front seats. I was so shocked by their sudden entrance; I wondered how close they were to us and if they saw what happened. Meanwhile, Gio was in his seat, looking immaculate as if he hadn't been mauling me a few seconds ago. In no time, Johnny was starting the car, and we were on the road.

"What just happened?" I said to Gio.

"What do you mean?"

"You know what I'm talking about." His smug evasiveness was irritating. We were about to have sex. I was still hot and aroused and he was sitting there, cool as a cucumber, seemingly unaffected.

"Are you talking about the make-out session we just had?"

My cheeks heated. I glanced at the front of the car. The two men's heads never moved, and they were staring straight at the road, but it didn't mean they didn't hear us. I pressed a button, and the partition went up. Gio chuckled. "What's so funny?" I asked. He only chuckled louder. "I wanted to prove a point," he said.

I was getting angrier and angrier. "And?"

He turned his entire body to face me. "Point proven. You're hot for me, regardless of your statements to the contrary. If I hadn't called my men, we would have fucked. Hell, I'm sure we can fuck now with them watching."

I was about to smack back with a retort of my own. I wanted to tell him to fuck off, or something similar, but the longer I thought about what he was saying, the more I realized he was at the very least bullshitting. He clearly was angry with me when he practically dragged me out of the gallery. And he had every right to be angry. I had acted horribly towards him. I never thought stealing money from him would impact him to the degree it did. And maybe this was the punishment, which I deserved, but I could tell it was something more. He was hurting, and he wanted me to hurt as well.

"I'm sorry," I said.

"I don't know what you're talking about?"

"You had a freaking yacht! I thought you had more money than to do with."

"It was a friend's. I was a caretaker and guest."

"If I had known…"

"You had what? Not stolen from me. Not scammed me? You want me to believe that?"

Had I known, would I have not done it? I would like to think so, but the people I was working with would not have let me. "I want you to forgive me."

"A little too late for forgiveness, don't you think?"

A pang hit my chest at the sound of those words. Why was I expecting forgiveness from a Morelli, anyway? They aren't known for their kind hearts and good deeds. Our relationship was fucked from the beginning, and trying to rectify the past was a fool's errand. "So, vengeance is what you chose," I said. "Is that what the little petting exercise was about?"

He shrugged. "I don't make any pretensions about being attracted to you." He's never said it outright and hearing him say it flipped something inside me. But he wasn't done. "I want to have sex with you. That was the only good thing to come out during that cursed time in Greece. I was a fool then, but my eyes are open now and I know who I am dealing with. It's you who acts like she's aloof. The little petting exercise was to show you that want me as much as I want you. As for the painting, my mother was the last person I was thinking about."

"So, it was just about sex only?"

"Yep."

He was lying, but the opening was now closed and I could not probe further. "Of course. I should have guessed," I replied.

He straightened back in his seat, and the conversation ended there. Part of me still wanted to show him I wasn't what he thought of me. I wanted him to know that I wasn't just a con artist who likes to party and sleep around whenever she's not swindling people. But the other part, the rational part, knew that whatever I would say would not matter. "Great, but you still stole from me," he would probably say. That would be true. He pretty much said the same thing in different words. My sin of conning him would not change. It would remain and so would his hatred. And who wanted to be loved by him, anyway? It was a naïve girl's wish, and I was not that.

The rest of the trip was silent, and we arrived at the apartment a few minutes later. The elevator ride to the penthouse was just as silent and awkward. By the time we entered the apartment, I was itching to say something. I broke the silence after we were left alone and pointed to the painting Mickey had placed against the wall and asked, "So what's special about it? You wanted it so badly you practically threatened Kevin to get it."

He was a few paces in front of me, and he replied without looking back, making his way towards the stairs. "Is that your way of attempting small talk?"

"I was just curious, that's all."

"Stay curious," he said and went upstairs.

The coldness in his voice said all that was needed to be said. The topic was off limits. And if it wasn't his tone that said it, the message was in his demeanor. After I was sure he was in his room, I made my way to my own and slept a dreamless sleep.

The following morning came sooner than I wanted it to. Gio was already dressed in a well cut dark blue suit and was sitting by the counter when I entered the kitchen. On the counter, next to a steaming hot coffee mug, was his phone, which he seemed to read on with concentrated interest. He was no doubt reading the paper or something similarly erudite. I couldn't picture him doom scrolling on social media.

"Ready for work?" I said. That's the best opening I could think of that wouldn't invoke last night's conversation. He looked up from his phone and a lock of his hair swooped down to his forehead. My insides wobbled. He had no right to look that hot.

"I was. Until now. Pack your bags."

"I think I'm going to require more than a command if you want me to do anything. Maybe an explanation, followed by a request. You know, something normal people do."

He sighed. "I do not have the patience to fight with you right now."

"You've gotta do better than that, buddy. If you're going somewhere, leave me here. I got stuff to do, anyway. I got a store to open, remember?"

"Simona," he said, raking his hair, "my brother's woman has been kidnapped, and we're going to the mattresses. You could either give me some grace and do as you're told for once, and maybe you won't get kidnapped as well."

"Your brother's *woman?* His girlfriend. The one he was with at the wedding?"

"I don't know if he would call her his girlfriend, personally I think she's more than that to him. What's important here is that we need to take you to a safe place or you're dead. Do you understand?"

The weight of his words slowly sank in. The war he was talking about last night had come. The reason he married me. Somehow, it didn't seem real until now. Part of me thought it would never come to this. That everyone was being overly cautious.

"What should I pack?" my voice was strained and shaky. He immediately softened when he no doubt saw the fear in my eyes. In a reassuring tone, he said, "Necessities. One bag. Nothing fancy."

"A—are they coming here?" I didn't need to explain who they were, and he seemed to understand. "No. I don't know. But we need to get you to a safe house, before any of his men who are in this city think of getting to us first."

"Right. Okay. Let me do that," I said and hurried back to my room.

Half an hour later, we were in the car park with Giovanni holding my bag. We were waiting for someone. I was too nervous to ask who. A few seconds later, a black car with black windows came through and stopped in front of us. The door opened and a muscular woman I've never seen before stepped out. She was wearing the same outfit I had seen Giovanni's men wear. Black pants, a shirt, and a jacket. Giovanni handed her my bag. "Get in," he said to me. I obliged. The woman got in after me, but Gio stayed put. "You're not coming?" I asked. He shook his head. "If you don't see me within in a month, she'll know what to do," he said. Nodding his head towards the woman, he said to her, "Remember my instructions." She replied with a gruff voice and that was it. The door was closed, and the car sped off, leaving Gio standing there and me being carried off to some unknown place in a car with strangers.

8

SIMONA

Never in my life did I think I would ever yearn for a man. Wonder if he was well. If he wasn't hurt. Or worse... dead. And yet, here I was, two weeks into isolation, wondering if Giovanni was alive or not. Whether he had succeeded in whatever mission he had gone to. He didn't tell me anything. He had put me into a car which had taken me to a safe house and left me there. His worried and agitated expression had been enough for me to do as he said, and now that same expression tormented me. It was funny how one can grow to miss someone they thought they hated.

My two bodyguards did not allow me to leave. They did not allow me a phone, laptop or any device that could access the Internet. For my protection, they said. They did not want to talk to me either, which meant I had to resort to the television and a Blu-ray DVD collection, courtesy of Gio apparently. For companionship, they said. How he knew the type of shows and movies I would want to watch is still a mystery, but a part of me thanked him for the foresight. It made the time less stressful, but the worry still niggled at the back of my mind every time I watched *Pretty Woman*.

Every day, I kept wondering if it was the day he would walk in to announce that it was over or if somebody else would walk in announcing he's dead. His death meant I would be free. Hell, even his success meant I would be free because of our agreement. Whatever the outcome, I would either end up a rich widow or a rich divorcee. And even that didn't make me happy. It was odd. I didn't care about him. I hated him. But I didn't want him to die.

Another horror plagued me. What if we were found out? Blake and Matteo assured me no one followed us here, and it was the best safe house in the country. They had gone above and beyond to make sure that even I didn't know where I was. They blindfolded me as soon as we were out of the city and at some point, placed noise-canceling headphones and gave me music to listen to. It was only after I entered the house that they removed them. The only thing I could tell is that it was a heavily secured farmhouse in the country. Even so, thoughts of his enemies bursting through the door and raining bullets on all of us plagued me all day and invaded my nightmares.

That was what my life was like for two weeks. Living with two introverts and watching series and movies while worrying about my husband.

Then, one day, the doorbell rang. The two bodyguards, both looked at each other. "Is it him?" I asked, getting up from the couch. Matteo, the man, put a finger on his mouth to tell me to be quiet while Blake, the woman, crouched silently towards the door. They both got their guns out at the same time. Oh god, I thought. Is this how I was going to die? In God knows where land, at the hand of some unknown enemy of my husband?

Three taps on the door came immediately after. The two looked at each other again. They seemed to relax a little, but they did not drop their guns.

Blake made cautious steps to the door as Matteo and I waited behind. As she peered through the peephole, I thought I saw her bulky shoulders relax. She then put her gun back in its holster and opened the door. Relief washed over me when I saw who it was. I didn't even think. I ran past Matteo and Blake and went straight to hug Giovanni. His familiar scent immediately enveloped me. Seeing him again unharmed made me want to embrace him for longer. The torment was over.

It took me a little too long to realize that he had not embraced me as well and remembering my surroundings and the state of our relationship; I let go of him, my cheeks reddening at the obvious display of affection. He went inside and Blake came over to close the door. Gio acknowledged the bodyguards, asked them if there were any anomalies, thanked them, and turned back to face me. His face was impassive, his emotions unclear. He could have been happy, sad, or distraught. I cleared my throat. I felt I had to say something, but nothing profound came to mind except for, "You're back."

"Yes," he said.

"Did," I stammered, "Did it go the way you wanted it to go?"

He raised an eyebrow. "If you're asking if we won, yes, we did."

I wondered what that meant. As I watched him command the two men to pack things up and get ready to leave, my thoughts kept wandering to an image of Giovanni, gun in hand, shooting mercilessly at faceless men. Did he kill people in order to win? He must have, right? He was part of 'the family' after all, if not practically the head of it. It was difficult to fully reconcile the suave wall street banker that was the Giovanni I knew and Giovanni the cold-blooded killer. It did not compute.

We left the safe house soon after. Gio and I got into the same car as Matteo and Blake while the car Gio came with had Mickey and Johnny following us. My heart swelled when I saw them. They seemed well and unharmed.

I was relieved to escape the oppressive atmosphere and get my phone back, but I was more concerned about the person next to me in the car than the unread messages. "What?" he asked, after he caught me sneaking a glance at him. Blake and Matteo were in front, and I felt too shy to ask what was on the tip of my tongue. Gio seemed to notice it and closed the partition. Even with the private space he had given me, getting out the specific words turned out to be more difficult. Instead of direct and clear questioning, I fumbled out a sentence saying, "When you said it's over, does that mean…"

"If you're going to ask a question, ask it fully." I can't believe I had forgotten what a jerk he could be. Two weeks I spent worrying over him only to remind me in less than a few hours who I was dealing with.

I tried again, a little more confident this time. "Does that mean you and I are no longer necessary?"

He burst out laughing. It must have been the first show of emotion I had seen in him since he came back. "It's not funny," I responded, irritated by his laughter. He made me feel like a stupid child. "You will not get rid of me that easily," he said. "Our agreement, which was made for the sake of my family's war with Saccone, is still in place even though the war is over." In a lower voice, he added, "I made sure of that."

"Why?"

"You know why."

I did, and his reason was irrational. I would probably do the same if I were in his shoes. However, he seemed to regard me as a nuisance most of the time. Tormenting me would be tormenting himself. "But do you really want this marriage?" I asked. "I'm sure you have plenty of women you want to be with who aren't me. Women who are more fun."

"I've been with plenty of women before. Most of them aren't fun. But watching you squirm is."

"I don't want to stay married to you!"

A small smile appeared on his features. It was in contrast to the realization of impending doom I was feeling and I wanted to wipe it off with a slap. "Is that why you were so happy to see me? You thought this would be the end of our relationship? And here I thought you missed me."

What's funny is that I had missed him. I had thought about him constantly to the point of having difficulty eating on some days. My heart had yearned for him and there was no way I was going to tell him that. The rational thing was not to live with this man, but to leave him. He didn't want me. I didn't want him. The condition on which we agreed the marriage upon had come to pass. The obvious thing to do was to terminate the marriage. "Of course," I lied. "Why wouldn't a woman trapped for a fortnight not be happy when she knows she would be free of the man who put her in that cage?"

He laughed. "That cage was for your benefit." I rolled my eyes. He ignored the gesture and said, "You should have read the fine print. Honestly, Simona, I thought you were smarter than that."

I thought I was and if this had been any normal arrangement with any other person, I would have read every word on that paper. However, this was Giovanni and I was too nervous to read carefully and too eager to please my father to ask whenever I encountered a term I didn't understand. I simply perused the contract and signed.

"I need to see the contract when we get back," I said.

"No need," he said before bending down to take out a tablet from his briefcase. He swiped a couple of times on it and handed it to me. "Here it is." On it was a scanned document of the contract, the one I signed. My signature was at the bottom of every page. I read it frantically until I reached the important part of the document. The part where it said, "The two parties will remain married for five years or longer if the earlier condition is met within five years." I don't remember reading this part. It was towards the end of the document, after all the frivolous stipulations of the wedding ceremony. At that point, I was flipping through the pages and not reading carefully. Fuck.

"Your father added that," Gio said after a while. "Something about grounding you, he said. But my Italian is poor, so I didn't catch exactly what he said."

Father had not liked my partying and other ancillary activities I got up too. His dislike had less to do with me and more to do with my mother. He thought she had led me astray, and he was right. He had always tried to find a way to keep me in check, and he might have finally succeeded. Resigned to my fate, I handed Gio the tablet, and he threw it back into his briefcase. We're still going to remain tethered to each other, I thought. I wasn't sure whether to be happy or sad. I was feeling both emotions.

"Saccone," I asked, "the person you were fighting is he not going to bother you—us anymore?" He straightened in his seat and turned to saying, "Yes."

"And you won?"

"If decimating one's entire operation, killing the head of said operation, and putting the pieces under our operation is winning, then yes, we did," he responded.

I barely cared about the unsavory part of the 'business', but even I knew the Saccone family was powerful. They were or had been one largest Mafia family in the world and its dismantlement meant that the Morelli family was now the biggest and most powerful. It was a scary prospect. This man, my avowed enemy, my husband for the next five years at least, was now one of the most powerful men in the world.

9

SIMONA

Even though I was back in a familiar place, I still felt suffocated. How does one get back to normal after going into fear mode for two straight weeks? My husband, the only person I knew who could answer the question, wasn't exactly forthcoming. We barely spoke to each other after we came back. He was just as busy as before and ignoring me like before. If he wasn't going to help me, I was going to help myself by emulating him. I tried to focus on my stuff. Trying to get my business off the ground. It worked at first. I made a plan of what I needed to do and looked at locations for my store and designed the interior, doing it all online. It wasn't safe for me to move around yet, according to Gio. There were still threats on my life and his, and I couldn't stray too far from the penthouse until he was sure I was safe. The continued restriction only made the claustrophobia worse. Two more weeks passed like this and by the end, I could not take it anymore. I was dying to get out. I wanted to go somewhere, anywhere. It was a bright Friday afternoon and when I went to look at the view of the park; the greenery called on me to come. So, I did. I put on my best flowy sundress and went downstairs.

When I got out of the elevator, a stern Mickey and a bored Johnny immediately got up from their seats in the lobby. "Going to the coffee shop?" Mickey asked. The two men, like Gio, did not look like they had survived a gang war. They appeared casual and unaffected. My only job had been to stay put, but it seemed as if I was the one who had gone through it.

"No. The park."

Mickey and Johnny glanced at each other.

"I don't think—" Mickey started.

"I don't care what he told you Mickey, I need

to get out and you two are going to follow me."

Johnny looked a little worried. I could tell he was searching for a way to dissuade me, but also knew he would be fighting a losing battle. "The coffee shop, the bookshop and the—"

"Chanel store are the only places I'm supposed to go. Well, fuck that. It's the park today boys," I said and marched out of the building and into the sun. I soaked it up as it warmed my cold skin. My pores opened as a breeze passed by. I could feel the clutches loosen.

"Mrs. Morelli." I sighed. Mickey rushed over to block my path but since he couldn't be too aggressive, I easily side-stepped him and continued walking.

"I don't think you should do this, Mrs. Morelli," he said as he came to walk beside me. I could hear Johnny's footsteps behind me as well, although he kept his usual distance.

"What happened to Simona?" I asked without sparing him a glance.

"Mr. Morelli told us to call you by your formal name."

"Well, I'm tired of doing what Mr. Morelli says. My name is Simona and I'm going into the park." I strolled down the street and as I was about to pass by a building under construction, Mickey blocked me. This time he was successful because of the scaffolding narrowing the path. I turned around only to face Johnny, blocking the other side.

"Fuck it, you know what? Let me call him." I took out my phone, dialed his number, and waited. I could make a run for it, I thought. But Johnny looked nimble and athletic. He could probably catch me. The humiliation of being brought back arms behind my back was too much for me to attempt that. After when I thought it would ring forever, he answered. "Your babysitters are being a nuisance," I said as soon as he picked up.

"Now why do I have the suspicion that it's the opposite?"

"A walk in the park should be, you know, a walk in the park."

"Not anymore, it's not. There are people after me and they're probably after you too, so it's sort of necessary to stay put if you want to keep your pretty head."

"If I stay one more second in that building, I just might jump to get out. I'm dying for air."

"Simona," he said, sighing.

"Gio," I challenged him. There was a long silence at the other end and for a moment I thought he had hung up until he said, "Give Mickey the phone."

I huffed and waved the phone at the bulky man. He took it and gave me his back as he spoke. I couldn't hear what Gio was saying, Mickey only responded with grunts, and after he was done, he handed it back to me. Gio was still on the line. "Take your walk, but I told them to keep their distance."

"Thank you," I said and ended the call.

After it was settled, Mickey resumed walking three feet in front of me and Johnny resumed walking three feet behind me. The city was no longer as crowded as it usually was during the morning rush, and it made walking easier.

When I entered the park, I slowed my walk down to a leisurely stroll and breathed in the fresh air. I was feeling free again. The invisible binds in my mind, slowly untangling. There was something about weekday afternoons, in particular this one, that I like. The bright sun, the warm weather that wasn't too hot, or too cold it was just right. I closed my eyes and took it all in. The cool breeze, the warm sun the—I bumped into something that felt like steel and rubber. My eyes flashed open in time to see a cycler fall to the ground with her bike on top of her right in front of me. Fuck! I rushed over to her, afraid she had sustained injuries. "Oh, I'm sorry!" I said as I tried to help her up. "I wasn't looking."

She didn't look like your typical biker. Not with her pink and white beach cruiser that matched her distinct candy pink helmet and white floral dress. As she was brushing off dirt from her dress, I lifted her bicycle from the ground. One handle was broken, and the chain had dislocated. From the corner of my eye, I saw Mickey closing the distance, looking concerned, and I discreetly gave him a thumbs up to stay away.

"Are you okay?" I asked the cyclist. She finished wiping off dirt off her dress and straightened. She looked to be about my age and had a heart-shaped pretty face and voluminous brunette hair that fell to her shoulders. As if I wasn't already feeling bad, her bruised cheek made me feel even worse. "I'm so sorry," I added.

"Oh, it's fine. Your hand, however." She pointed to a scratch on the side of my left hand. I didn't realize I was injured until she pointed it out. It had a bruise, but it wasn't bleeding. Her bruise, however, looked like it would swell.

"You should let me help you clean your wound. My place is nearby," I said.

"It's fine," she said, taking her bike, but as she did, she stumbled and I had to hold her before she fell.

"Let me help," I said and gestured to Mickey

to come over. Johnny got up from the bench where he was sitting and also made his way over.

"My friends and I can help you to my apartment and I can take care of that wound. It's the least I can do."

She looked around and saw the two men coming over. "If I'm not putting you out of your way?"

"Not at all," I said to her as Johnny took hold of her bike and started fixing it. There was nothing that could be done about the handle, but the chain could be restored.

"Mrs. — I mean Simona," Mickey said, drawing me away from the woman. "What is it?" I said to him. "I don't think we should bring strangers to the apartment,"

"Oh come on. Do you think she's a spy?"

He shrugged.

"Well, I don't think she is. Besides, I thought I was the one who makes the calls here?"

"Craig has a first aid kit."

That sounded like a good enough compromise. Taking her to the concierge desk was just as good and didn't make me feel like a moron for leaving her alone after causing the accident. "Fine," I conceded.

Mickey went over to the woman and held her by the waist to help her walk, while Johnny took the bicycle. It looked like she might have bruised her knees as well. "Thank you," the woman said as we helped her to the apartment building. When we arrived, Mickey and I settled her down onto one of chairs while Johnny went over to Craig to ask for a first aid kit.

"You really shouldn't have done this," the woman said again.

"If it makes you feel better, I'm only doing this to make myself feel better."

She chuckled. Mickey came with the kit and some towels which I used to dress the woman's wounds. After I was done, I helped her stand, and she thanked me once again. "Do you want to grab a cup of coffee?" she asked. Coffee? "Since you went above and beyond, now I feel like I should thank you." I wasn't thinking about spending some time with her any longer, but now that she suggested it, I was down. "Sure, why not?"

A few minutes later, we were sitting in the cafe two blocks down, with lattes in our hands. Mickey and Johnny were three tables away, sticking out like two sore thumbs, but it didn't bother me. Allison, her name was Allison, was so cool and interesting and kept entertaining me with fun stories. We came in for a cup of coffee and an awkward chat and ended up ordering two slices of cakes, more coffee and having a pleasant afternoon with a stranger.

After finishing one story about her college hijinks, Allison said, whilst glancing over at my two bodyguards, "Sorry to ask, but are you famous?" I shook my head, knowing why she was asking.

"I only ask because of your…"

"It's a long story. My husband is important, that's why."

"H-husband?" Her demeanor, which had been bright all along, darkened for a second and I thought I saw a wash of sadness, but then she brightened again. I thought it odd, maybe I misread it.

I put up my hand and wiggled my ring finger, showing her the diamond ring. "Newly married," I said to her. She took my hand and inspected the ring. "Wow. I figured you were rich, but you must be rich rich. "

"My husband is." Gio is practically a billionaire, but telling her that somehow felt like bragging.

Allison continued to examine the ring, titling my hand to the light like a jeweler. She could not look away and the longer she held my hand, the tighter the hold got until I snatched it away from her grasp.

I was no longer feeling like I was with an old friend. The mood had shifted. We were back to being strangers again. The hairs on the back of my neck rose in warning. Whatever my instincts were warning me about, I didn't know, but I decided to follow them, "I think I should leave," I said. I didn't have anywhere to go except back to the apartment, but that felt better than being here.

"Did I do something wrong?" Her tone sounded sweet and apologetic, and it made me feel rude. I shook my head. "No. It's just that I had a thing planned and I might miss it if I linger for too long."

"Of course, of course. We should do this again sometime," she said, "The coffee, that is. Not the accident." Her mouth widened with a bright smile. Guilt washed over me again and, feeling like I should atone for my wrong doing I asked, "We should trade numbers? You know, so we could stay in touch."

She beamed again. "That would be great."

I wanted to return her smile, but I couldn't. Even as I took out my phone and gave her my number, an irrational part of me wanted to reverse the act. Because it felt like I had just made a mistake.

10

GIOVANNI

Five years ago

She was a dream. I could not believe that someone could be so beautiful both inside and outside. She was full of vigor and life. Her intellect was another pleasant surprise. A woman like her was a rare gem. We must have been on the beach for hours. I was so rapt in our conversation; I failed to notice the sun descending, and it was only after she mentioned it was getting dark that I looked around us and noticed we were the only ones left.

I had approached her merely as a beauty to be conquered. A woman to keep my bed warm for a night or two while I was in Greece. She had all the right attributes. A girl looking for fun, a body made for sin and tits to drown in. And yet I wanted more. I wanted her to be more than a fling, and that was only after talking to her for a few hours. In that short time, I had learned a lot about her. She was on the island with friends. They were celebrating graduation and were hoping to enter the fashion industry soon after. During our conversation, she had let it slip that her family was in the 'business'. I'm not sure she noticed she did. I was accustomed to taking hints from people's conversation and putting two and two together when it came to the mafia world. Her name was Simona Vannucci, and she was originally from Italy where most of her family still was, but she grew up in the United States with her mother. That was a big hint. I knew of a Vannucci Mafia Family headed by a man in Tuscany. He had sons. I didn't know he had a daughter, though the surname, a somewhat common one, could have been a coincidence. The hint that sealed it was when she said her father was in the import/export business. That was enough for me.

Vannucci was a known arms dealer and no one who was legally importing and exporting things called it the 'import/export business'.

One of my rules was not dating anyone connected to that side of the world and instead of dropping her and moving on, I was tempted to break my rule. It's not like she was in the business, just tangentially tied to it.

"Do you care to join me for dinner?" I said as we got up. "I don't want to intrude on what you and your friends will do, of course."

"Oh, don't worry about them." She rolled her eyes and puffed her chest in a sexy way that tightened my groin even more. "They'll want to take me clubbing. Rubbing against strangers' bodies while dangling a drink in hand doesn't feel like how I want to spend my night today."

My heart leapt at the prospect of spending more time with her. A few hours hadn't been enough. "So it's a date, then?" I tried to keep my voice even and not come off as over eager.

"Is it?"

Fuck. Was I over eager? "If you want it to be?"

"I'm in room eighty-nine," she said with a sweet smile and got up. She walked away as the sun set, her skin glowing in the waning light. I didn't know it, but I was well and truly fucked.

Now.

The ballroom, while large and barely full, was suffocating. I could not stand the dozens of colognes and perfume filling my nostrils more than I could stand the constant ass kissing from men who wanted to move up the ranks. The women were no better. They could see I came with someone and many knew she was my wife and yet they could not stop eying me. Even Simona noticed and gave me a look of disdain, as if I was the one encouraging it. I didn't want to be here. My night would have been better if I were at the apartment with Simona under me. Or anywhere really, as long as I was deep inside her.

It's been a week since Simona and I had sex and I still wanted more. I should never had underestimated her addictive qualities. We spent most of our time in Santorini making love, after all. I thought my obsession with her would have cooled after five years. I was young and hotheaded back then. One would think that a more mature me would have better control over lustful impulses. However, I found myself over the past weeks thinking of her sweet body, how amazing being inside her felt and how powerful that orgasm was. It had been a while since I felt like that, I dared not count how long.

The two weeks we spent away from each other

had only inflamed my passion, not dampen it. I spent that period living on the edge. I was the more erudite of my family. Rico and Nico liked to call me a nerd. Shooting people and living in hiding was not my thing. Living like every day was my last, was not my thing. And now that Saccone was eliminated, the tense period I had gone through had only made me want Simona more. No wonder men fucked anything and everything after war back in the day. The fear of death made a man's blood run hot.

"Morelli!" The voice of a burly middle-aged man took me out of my thoughts. It was a longtime business partner of mine, the host himself, Ivanov. "How are you?" I said, offering a hand, but he gave me a hug instead, slapping my back hard twice. "I thought you said birthday parties were not your thing? What made you change your mind?"

"You're my friend. Why would I miss your daughter's birthday party?" Ivanov did not look like he bought it, but he was gracious enough to act otherwise.

"They grow so fast, don't they? Yesterday she was calling me 'papa'. Today she's saying 'Daddy, I need a big twenty-one birthday bash,' so I gave it to her." He punctuated his sentence with a laugh. Beside me, I felt Simona wince. I knew what she was thinking. There's no way a girl that young wanted to celebrate her birthday with her dad's old friends and business partners. This party was very much Ivanov's than it was his daughter's.

"And is this the lovely wife of yours I keep hearing about?" Ivanov said, taking Simona's hand in his. He said something in Russian and Simona replied, "That's for you to find out," snatching her hand away playfully. Ivanov laughed. "No wonder you married her. I was saving my daughter for you, but I see you found beauty, brains and wits all in one person."

"I'm a lucky man."

"That you are," he said as he was being interrupted by one of the service staff. "So glad you came. I hope we can chat more, but in the meantime, please enjoy," he turned his attention to the man and walked away with him

"I didn't know you spoke Russian," I said to Simona when we were alone again.

"Surprised I have more skills than you thought capable?"

"Oh no. I can never underestimate your capacity for hidden talents."

She shook her head. "You should get over it. It was five years ago."

"Am I supposed to forget that my darling little

wife is a con artist and thief who preys on men?"

"And yet you married me."

"Figured I can handle you. You need to kept away from impressionable men. I'm only doing a community service."

She huffed.

"Speechless for once?" Toying with her was fun. It made this dreary party exciting.

"That friend of yours seems a little creepy," she said, changing the subject.

Feeling protective suddenly, I asked, "Why? What did he say to you?"

"He came on to me."

Even though I didn't approve of Ivanov's actions, I tried to comfort her by saying, "He's a toothless dog. He likes to flirt with other peoples' wives and girlfriends, but he's ultimately harmless."

"Why are we here, anyway?" She asked her gaze darting around the room. "The idea of celebrating a twenty-first birthday party with geriatric people is not my idea of fun." I looked around. Simona and I were the few people here who were south of forty. I felt sorry for the poor kid. "Is it because you enjoy watching people fall over themselves to kiss your ring?"

"Ivanov is a longtime business partner of the Family. I have to attend to whatever silly function he invites me to keep him happy."

"So, what does he provide for you? Drugs? A sex trafficking ring?"

"You act as if you aren't part of this world when your own family is one of the oldest in the business. You're practically a blue blood."

She looked away from me to the dancefloor. A few people were dancing, and I took Simona's hand and led her to it. "Some of us didn't choose who we were born to," she said. Was that a crack I heard in her voice?

"I don't think anyone choses their parents," I replied as we started swaying to the slow and sensual music.

"You seem to enjoy your position as the head of the biggest Mafia family in the country."

"Enjoying is an overstatement. I merely accepted my lot in life. It's a pretty lot, after all. But you know," I said, twirling her in my arms in time with the music. "I never understood why you agreed to marry me. You know why I married you. Why did you sign the agreement?" We both swayed in time with the music. Our bodies were made for each other and were just as compatible on the dance floor as they were in bed. She danced in time with my steps, I with hers. There was a fluidity to our motions that I doubt I could replicate with another woman.

"You'll never understand," she said, shrugging, "so why bother?"

Her mood had shifted, and there was a slight, almost imperceptible scowl on her face. I felt an urge to kiss it away and ask what had made her frown so I can make it right. It made no sense. I should be the angry one here, not here. But my anger kept being defeated by a stronger emotion. The urge to remove the backless red dress she had on and have my way with her on this dancefloor. Or maybe not remove it. Instead, find a room, flip it up, rip her panties off and fuck her senseless. That's what I wanted to do to the person I hated the most. This desire I had for her had to be tempered. If she were ever to know the hold she had on me, I would be done for. I had to expend it before that happened.

"Whatever," I said. "I don't care, as long as you put up with your end of the deal. I hope you've read up on the contract again since last time." Her face lit up with a smile, but there was an unsettling, mischievous glint in her eye. "There's a—"

"Gio?" I turned to the source of the familiar voice. A tall, thin blond in a shimmering silver dress was standing behind us. We stopped dancing, but I kept Simona in my arms. "Irina? I thought you were in London?" The last time we met was in her Chelsea apartment where Irina and I had breakup sex. That was after I heard she was telling anyone who would listen that she and I were soon to be married. Self-confidence was not a thing she lacked, something I liked in her, but if there was something like too much self-esteem, she had it. We were never serious, and I thought I was clear to her it was just a fling. However, even after I told her we should break up, she didn't seem to understand that it was for good.

"The agency wanted me in New York, so here I am."

"A promotion?"

"Lateral move not that I'm complaining. New York is your home, after all. This time, I'll be closer to you." Irina lowered her voice as she spoke the last sentence, placing innuendo that removed any doubts to the implication of her words. I felt Simona stiffen beside me. "When I heard that Ivanov was throwing a party," she continued in a higher tone, "I knew you would be here." Irina leaned in to whisper something, but just before she uttered a single word, Simona cleared her throat. Irina's gaze shifted to hers. She gave Simona one of her typical dismissal smiles. Damn, she was going to make this harder for me.

"Irina, say hello to my wife, Simona. Simona," I drew her unyielding body closer to me, "Irina. An old friend."

Irina's smile faltered for a second before she plastered it back again. "Wife? I had no idea you'd found someone, let alone gotten married."

"It was a whirlwind romance," Simona said.

"Oh," Irina's eyebrows arched. "I never took Giovanni Morelli as the type of person to fall in love. He's always been a lone wolf."

Simona encircled her arm around mine and added, "We rekindled an old romance and found out that we loved each other still."

"Charming," Irina said. The word sounding like ash dripping from her mouth. She gave me a tight smile and saw, or pretended to see, a friend of hers and soon left us.

I turned to Simona. "Whirlwind romance? Found each other?"

"What? I thought you wanted everyone to think this is a genuine marriage? Did I not make it real enough for you?"

"I just find it funny that you went from a dead log to a clingy and possessive creature when she came along."

"Your supermodel girlfriend seemed to think you're still available. I had to warn her you're off the market the best way I could. We agreed not to see other people, right?"

"She's not a supermodel. She's a lawyer who's represented fortune five hundred companies. And she was never my girlfriend."

"Is that why she was practically leaning into you whenever she spoke?"

"You sound bothered."

"That's because all the women here are wondering why their favorite catch is with someone new. I have to let them know you're off the market or they'll start hounding you."

"You're doing this for me?" I said in a mocking tone. "That's sweet."

"I'm doing it for myself. I don't want to be humiliated. And end whatever relationship you and Irina have. You can't fuck outside the marriage if I can't."

"Damn. You're jealous." She couldn't hide the blush much as she tried to cover her face with her hair. "Don't worry, she's not that special and what we had was over before we got married."

"Sure. Whatever."

I wondered if she was truly jealous or if she was merely putting me off her scent. It's not as if she wasn't receiving attention at all. Far from it. Ever since we came in, every man in the room has been taking every opportunity they can to steal a glance at her or ogle from a distance. It was why

I was making sure she did not leave my side. She was making me possessive.

I was about to reassure Simona further about Irina when I felt her stiffen. She looked like she had seen a ghost. I followed her gaze, which was fixed on a middle-aged man, possibly in his forties, who seemed unremarkable if it weren't for a familiarity in his features. I had a sense I had seen him before, but I wasn't sure.

"One of your friends?" I asked her.

She cleared her throat and straightened her posture. When she turned to face me, the fear was gone, replaced with a poor imitation of nonchalance. "Former friend."

"Just a friend?"

"Of sorts."

"A night of coincidences, it seems."

I watched as this friend of sorts made his way into the ballroom with a woman old enough to be his daughter on his arm. He seemed well known to some people in the crowd, including the birthday girl. Simona turned her entire body to face me and away from him, as if she was hiding. That piqued my interest. "Do you still want to stay here? I'm feeling a little sick," she said. Now that made me more curious. "Why? We only just got here," I said. "Fine. I'll go." She wriggled out of my embrace, taking a few steps towards the exit. "Oh, come on," I said, drawing her back. "You met my ex. It's only fair I meet yours." Her eyes widened.

Was this her partner in crime? I wondered. That could be it. Maybe they had a falling out. There's no honor among thieves, after all. Simona tried again to wriggle out of my arm, but I wouldn't let her. Even if she wanted to leave, the couple had already spotted us and were making their way towards us. "Isn't it funny how we're always bumping into your *friends* whenever we go out?"

"Funny for you, maybe. Not me."

"Is he another victim of yours? Is that why you don't want us to meet? Afraid we'll compare notes." She glared at me. "No."

"So it is your partner in crime. I knew it."

She looked like she wanted to say something, but she was cut off by a joyful greeting.

"I knew it was you!" The man said.

Simona, who was apprehensive before, put on a big plastic smile and said, "Oh my god, Terry, surprised to see you!" She gave him and the woman he was with both a light hug and air kisses. The de rigueur of fake greetings. She seemed happier to see her artist friend more than she did this Terry guy, whoever he was. What was with her and her friends? She seemed like she didn't like any of them. Well, the ones I had met so far, at least. Terry, on the other hand hadn't caught onto the fakeness on display. He extended his hand to me and introduced himself. "Terrence Bradley. Nice to meet you, Giovanni Morelli. My friends call me Terry." He chuckled. Mister two first names was shorter than I was, significantly so, and shook my hand with a tight grip that felt practiced. Like he learned it at some alpha male seminar in some lesson on how to exert dominance or some crap like that.

"You know me?" It's not like I was unknown, but he didn't seem like the usual wall street guys nor did he look like he was in the criminal world.

"Of course I do. Who doesn't around here?" He chuckled again, showing his artificially white teeth. I disliked him in that instant. There was a sliminess to him that raised my hairs. Add to that, Simona had frozen in my hold. She felt so stiff. I unconsciously rubbed her back to soothe her.

"So you and Morelli huh?" He said to Simona. She shrugged in what I'm sure everyone perceived as nonchalant, but I could feel the tension within her that it was anything but. "I knew you'd land on your feet eventually," he added. Simona cracked a smile and said nothing more. Terrance, or Terry, got the hint that she didn't want to talk, so he said, "It's been nice meeting you again. And you too Morelli." He took out a card from his pocket and handed it to me. It was black, with the words 'Terrance Bradley, CEO of Bradley Fund,' embossed in gold. So a wall street guy, then. "You and I should talk sometime." He slapped my shoulder and moved on together with his friend. As he was walking away, I realized he had never introduced us to the woman he was with.

"Care to explain your stiffness," I said after they were out of earshot.

She rolled her eyes. "Like you care. You would think I'm lying so why bother."

"Now I'm curious. I already think the worst of you. I doubt any new information would make my opinion of you sink any lower."

"Great. Just as I suspected."

"Well, spit it out. The curiosity is eating at me."

She took a deep breath and shook her head, as if deciding to throw caution to the wind. Finally, she said, "He was my pimp."

11

SIMONA

Five years ago

It was like being in a dreamland. When he came to my room and told me we would have dinner somewhere close to the hotel, I thought it would be a restaurant. Turns out it was a yacht. His freaking yacht. It was a beautiful boat, tastefully furnished and not at as tacky as some boats I've been on, not that I've been on many. Dinner was being served on the deck of the ship under the warm, starlit night sky. It could not be more romantic. Gio, as he liked to be called, was the best date to be with, yacht withstanding. He was attentive. Never presuming what I wanted, always making sure I was comfortable or enjoying my meal. When a light wind came through, Gio suggested we go inside and by then we had finished eating and were now drinking an old, no doubt expensive wine. I followed him into a cabin with white sofas and a view of the ocean and sky. We both sat on the same couch. I had wanted to be closer to him all night and now we were mere inches away from each other.

"You never told me what you do," I asked after we had run out of conversation. He had told me a lot about his family, his brothers, and his travels. He sounded like he traveled a lot. "You seem to be constantly moving from place to place and never sitting down."

"That's only because our business is in flux at the moment."

I gazed around. "I would not have guessed."

He chuckled. "Not everything you see is real."

"You're telling me this is not yours?"

"Appearances can be deceptive. I'm trying to keep my family's money. In fact, that's why I'm traveling so much." He shifted to face me. His gaze was so intense, it was like being under a microscope. "And what about you? You talked about working. I thought you were still in college. What kind of work do you do?"

I couldn't tell him the truth. I made a mistake when the word 'work' slipped out while I was relating a story. There's no way I would tell him what I really did, but I could tell him what I wanted to do. It's not as if I was ever going to meet this man again. We were from different worlds and somehow had collided into each other. From the surroundings, his manner of speech, and his general demeanor, he was clearly an old money type. While I was from the criminal underworld. "I'm a fashion designer. Well, aspiring fashion designer. I'm currently working for a small fashion house." The lie slid out so smoothly I didn't even have to think about it. But then again, it wasn't the first time I had used it. I just never used it with someone I liked.

Now

I never thought I could shake Giovanni's foundation until then. When I told him that Terry, or Slimy Terry as I liked to call him, was my pimp, his jaw dropped, he froze and when he finally gathered himself, his gaze darted around us as if he was shocked by his own reaction.

"You certainly hold a lot of secrets. A pimp. You're right, I wasn't expecting that." He shook his head. "But why?"

"What? Not a sophisticated enough line of work for you?"

"No. One would think a mafia princess would have enough money to not have to resort to sex work in order to get by. Unless you liked it, of course."

"It wasn't like that." I wanted our relationship to be as superficial as possible and telling him about Terry would let him in. If I let him, he would destroy me. I could not let that happen. "I know you like to call me princess, but my life was far from grand."

He took a sip of his champagne. "What was it like then?"

"Very different from yours, let's just say."

"If you had to whore yourself out for that guy—"

"It wasn't like that. I know I called him my pimp, but I did not have to sleep with men. Don't worry, you did not buy 'damaged goods'."

"Come on. I wasn't thinking like that at all. It's just that he was a little creepy and you were a lot stiffer than usual." He was leaning in closer and caressing my back as he spoke in what anyone who didn't know our relationship was like, would interpret as caring. Even I was in danger of forgetting that as well. His hand was too soft, too smooth.

"So you were concerned? Is that what you're trying to say?"

"It may surprise you, but yes."

"Sure." I desisted from rolling my eyes. His soft tone when he asked, "Was he horrible to you?" That had me doubting my convictions. If he truly was sincere, telling him the truth might be a good thing. But he could look for something to use against me later and, frankly, that was the most likely scenario. "He was bad," I said, "But not in the way you think and before you give me your fake pity, I was no victim."

Concern immediately turned to disgust. My heart plunged. I wanted any other emotion from him that wasn't his usual hate and seeing him switch back to normal hurt. But if I was honest with myself, that was the better emotion to deal with. A caring Giovanni was unsettling, and I prayed he never made a return.

"Of course," he said, "A woman like you is no one's victim. You are a predator. I don't know why I thought otherwise."

"Predator. You say that as if you aren't one yourself."

He scoffed. "Touché." His eyes went dark. "Is

that why you came after me? Because I was a predator?"

"Believe it or not, I didn't know who you were." I never gave a thought about what he did when we first met. He was a diversion from the dangerous game I was playing and I liked that he was nothing like the men I've known before. Fun, charming, and unassuming. He had been so eager to please me. It was refreshing, because I was usually the one playing that role. The time I spent with him before everything went to shit was the best I've ever been with someone. Hell, I didn't know he was rich until he took me to his yacht. I was on vacation when we met, not working. Then my mother found out who I was with. Then she told Terry. And everything changed.

"So you're telling me you stumbled onto me by accident? Our meeting was simply kismet? Two people drawn together by fate?"

"You're the one who came onto me first, remember?"

His eyes narrowed. Whatever else happened after, even he couldn't refute that he was the one to approach me and not the other way around. The change in Giovanni's face seem to show he was conceding to the fact. It was a small short-lived victory because his mood quickly shifted. He downed the rest of his drink and placed the glass on the tray of a passing server. He turned around to face me and pulled me within his grasp. Just at that moment, someone bumped into me behind me, pushing me against Gio. I gasped, shocked at the sudden movement and the electric current running up and down my spine at the thought of embracing him so close in a public place.

I heard glass, liquid, and metal crashing to the ground behind me, and that's when I realized a server had tripped and fell. The contents of his tray were on the floor. A cocktail of champagne, canapes, and broken glass. "Are you okay?" Gio asked. I nodded. "Your dress." I followed his gaze. The hem of my dress was soaking up the wine. Gio whisked me away from the mess, but he was a little too late. Some canapes had gotten into my dress. The server noticed this at the same time as I did and he muttered a few strangled worries as he straightened up awkwardly. I accepted his rambling apologies. The dress wasn't that damaged, and the material was easy to wash.

"We should get you cleaned," Gio said, his brow furrowed as he inspected my dress.

I gently swiped away his hand that trailing down my hip as he assessed the damage. Not because he was irritating me. Quite the opposite;

his touch made me feel hot. "Don't worry," I said to him, "it's fine." Before I could say more, he led me away from the mess and towards the bathrooms. There were several powder rooms, most of them unoccupied. We got into one, which had two empty stalls and a washbasin. Gio drew me to the counter and immediately went to work brushing off the bits of crumbs, meat, vegetables, glass, and wine off me with a wet paper towel. His actions were mechanical, but my body reacted with incendiary heat on every part he brushed. As he got lower and got onto his knees, my mind could not help wander what would happen if he were to ditch the towel, lift the dress and pull my thighs to his mouth. "See," I said after he was done cleaning the mess. My voice sounded a little too husky, so I cleared my throat before he caught onto the fact that what he was doing was arousing me. "It wasn't that big of a deal."

He straightened up and threw the towel into a nearby bin and rinsed his hands. "Yes, but the glass could have hurt you."

I rolled my eyes. "As if you care."

His gaze was intense when he stared at me. "I care enough to not want to see you hurt. Physically, at least." His voice was low. Almost seductive. It was disarming. I could sense the shift in the atmosphere. Suddenly, the surroundings felt intimate. The music in the hall beyond, quiet. My focus became him, as his was no doubt me. My gaze went to his mouth. The last time we kissed was a while ago. Just after he went away. We haven't done anything intimate since then. We haven't even been this close. I wonder why? Did he find a girlfriend during that time? Maybe he had a new woman who was less combative and did everything he said without question. That would certainly explain his distance with me. "What's on your mind?" he asked.

I blurt it out without thinking. "Where you with someone else? When you were gone."

He frowned. "Someone else?"

I felt like an insecure wife who could not stand the thought of her husband being away from her for five minutes. I did not like who I was becoming, but the lack of knowledge was gnawing at me. "A girlfriend."

"The only people I was with were my brothers and my brothers only. And sometimes some of my men, but that's it." A wave of relief washed over me.

"What were you doing there?" I noticed a speck of green on his shirt. It must have splattered on to it from the accident. I brushed it off, but my hand lingered.

"Managing Dante's business while he took care of business."

"Funny." He didn't need to explain it fully I understood what he was saying. While Dante was dealing with Saccone, Gio was running the casino, the place where the bulk of the Morelli fortune is generated.

Gio took hold of the hand that was on his chest and pressed it against his beating heart. "Do you think I'm lying?" I shook my head. Somehow, I knew he was telling the truth. It could have been in the way he said it. He spoke in a manner of someone confident in his answer while simultaneously amused by the question. As if the mere idea of him being with another person was ludicrous. But it wasn't for me. I had seen the way most of the women in that ballroom had devoured him just with their gaze. Their desire was shameless. I was positive I saw one woman brushing herself against him as we strolled past her. He had me by his arm, but they all acted like I was a temporary fixture.

"It's just odd," I said, "that someone like you would not have, you know, wandered."

"Someone like me?"

"Don't act so obtuse. I'm aware of your appetites."

He took hold of my chin and drew me close.

My pulse sped up. "My appetites, as you call them, are specific. I don't just go for anyone." I tried not to focus on what his words might mean. He surely wasn't saying I was the only woman he wanted. I was not that naïve. "How specific?" I asked, and I almost wanted to take it back because there was only one answer that would satisfy me and any other answer would not do. His mouth turned up slightly and softly he said, "You idiot," and took my mouth to his.

Our conversation melted away to nothing at the touch of his lips. I clung to him as if we had not done this in years when it was only a fortnight. His mouth was like magic as it brushed against mine. It could draw out desires I strove to bury with a simple kiss. I leaned into him, wanting more, and felt the pressure of his groin against mine. It was so erotically sweet; I ground against him, the need to feel him inside me growing. He lifted my leg and swung it around his waist. I lifted the other leg and did the same. We both moaned when I felt his cock against my wet center.

This is what I had been missing. Just a few weeks away from him and I was craving Gio like a drug. Dry humping wasn't enough. I wanted him. His cock. My hands went to his pants, and I fumbled with the zipper. A few quick and jerky movements later, his cock was free. It was hard, thick, and weeping to be inside me. I brushed off the pre-cum with my thumb and licked my finger. His eyes were cloudy with desire as they locked with mine. For a moment, time seemed to stop as we challenged each other to take the next step. Then he galvanized into action. He pushed me back against the wall, flipped up my dress, and ripped my underwear off. His cock entered me with a thrust so deep it pushed me up against the mirror with its force. I moaned a little too loudly, and he put a hand on my mouth to quiet me. His other hand went down to my clit, where he massaged it in time with his rhythmic thrusts. It was quick, but no less pleasurable. In no time, I could feel myself going over that edge and when I did, I screamed against his mouth as my pussy milked his cock. If he hadn't been covering my screams, I'm sure everyone in the ballroom would have heard us.

Gio was not too far behind. A couple more strokes and he flooded my pussy with his come. His head fell to my shoulder and bit down a moan against my neck. He must have made a mark there. A primitive part of me hoped he did. It was the part that wanted to be marked by him and display that mark to the world. I didn't know what to make of that odd desire, but I didn't have time to dwell on it. We were like that for a couple of minutes as we tried to snatch back our breaths and our sanity. Finally, Gio pulled back and stood to face me. His hair was disheveled and there were small beads of sweat on his forehead. He looked cute in that post orgasmic phase we were in. I had an urge to draw him in and kiss him, but the closer I observed, the more I noticed he wasn't in the same mood as I was. Something had changed within those few seconds and I could only describe the look on his face in one word; regret.

What the fuck do I know? I must have said out loud because he then said, "Fix yourself up and let's get out of here."

12

GIOVANNI

Five years ago

The sex was amazing. Probably the best I've ever had. I kept reaching for her throughout the night and each time we came together was better than the last. She was so responsive and in tune to what I wanted in an almost telepathic mode. And she was such a pleasure to please. I wanted her to enjoy the act as much as I was. I wanted to hear her cries of ecstasy. They were an aphrodisiac all on their own. By the time the sun came up, we had made love so many times that I had lost count. And when I woke up, it was to her scent filling my nostrils and her limbs entangled with mine in restful slumber. My gaze swept over her as she slept and remember thinking, I would love waking up like this every day. It was a thought that came out of nowhere and any other time, I would have jumped out of bed and kicked her out. But not that day. That morning, it was a comforting feeling. It was the first time I wanted to spend my life with someone and we had just met. It should not make sense, but somehow, on that day, with her, it did. The feeling was exhilarating. So much so I did the unthinkable. I pulled her closer to my chest and wrapped her in my arms. I was snuggling. Giovanni Morelli does not and has never snuggled with any woman *ever*. It felt good. I wanted to do it more often. Simona had flipped something within me. I liked it.

Two weeks later

I came back to the penthouse to be greeted by the hustle and bustle of people running around the apartment. The living room was a mess, with clothes, fabric, and garment bags strewn all around. A woman pushing a rack of clothes rushed past me, not even noticing that I was standing there. Even Mickey and Johnny were busy removing clothes from bags. And amidst all the chaos was Simona. She was in the middle of the room giving orders to a woman in black thick-rimmed glasses who was furiously noting down on a tablet.

"What's going on?" I was so puzzled I couldn't sum up any anger. I was more curious than anything else, but the room went quiet and all attention turned to me, then swiveled to Simona. She glanced up and in my direction. She frowned, as if surprised to see me, which was odd because I had told her I would be coming. My business deal ended up not taking longer than I originally thought and came back home earlier.

"You're back already?" she asked. "Why didn't you say you were coming?" She didn't even look the slightest bit guilty. I caught her turning our apartment into what one can only call a fashion disaster zone, but was instead interrogating me about coming back to my home. The audacity.

"I sent you a text. Are you converting the apartment into a shopping mall?" I made my way to her, kicking away some boxes and paper bags on the floor. My anger slowly building. Everyone else went back to their business as if nothing else had occurred. Mickey and Johnny at least had the decency to be embarrassed and dropped whatever they were doing. Simona, on the other hand, was acting as if all of this was normal. Nonchalantly, she replied. "Sorry, I was busy. I didn't see it. As for the mess, the store is being renovated, and the clothes came too early and everything needs to be organized so…" she shrugged, leaving the sentence hanging. As if the obvious answer was to bring hoards of people to my apartment.

"Can I talk to you for a second?" I didn't wait for her to answer. I grabbed her hand and all but dragged her out of the room. She didn't resist. We went to the first room I could think of, which was the study, and closed the door behind us.

"What the fuck are you thinking?"

"Nice greeting. Not even how are you? Just straight into," she put on a mocking tone, "What are you thinking? What's going on?"

"Both reasonable questions to someone finding out their home has been invaded by a fabric godzilla. Do you even understand who you're married to? The danger you've put us in. Do I need to explain it to you again!" I didn't mean to shout, but I ended up raising my voice the longer she stared at me with incredulity. As if I was the crazy one.

"Come on. They were all vetted. I don't think any of them are plotting to assassinate you in your sleep."

I closed my eyes and rubbed my temple, feeling a slight headache coming on. "Can you act like someone from your background for one second? Why the fuck are you bringing in strangers in our home?"

She rolled her eyes. "Like I said, the store is being renovated and we need a place to organize the clothes I ordered. I'm sorry they got in your way while you were not even around."

"Can you not act like a child and listen to what I'm saying, like an adult?"

Now it was her turn to raise her voice. "You're being anal! I told you, everyone's vetted. They're not going to steal your shit or kill you, okay! God!" she marched towards the door. I blocked her. "Where are you going?"

Arms akimbo, she said, "To tell them to leave. Isn't that what you want?" She bit her lip. It was not supposed to be sexy, but it was to me and for a second, I forgot I was angry with her. For only a second. "The two weeks you were away were the best time I had ever had, by the way. I wish you never came back."

"Really. I remember you rushing into my arms the last time I left for a similar period."

"That was before I realized how much of a dick you are. Something which you're proving now."

She bit her lip again. What was it about her? I was angry at her for not just exposing me, but exposing herself to danger. I was tired and jet lagged from a long trip. And yet all I could think of now was how much I wanted to have sex with her. It was ridiculous considering I had left for precisely that reason. I chose to go do a deal any of my underlings could have done because I wanted some time away from her. I left the morning after the party because I didn't like how I felt. She had turned me into a sex obsessed freak, something that I am not. Whenever she was in my presence, I could not think of anything else. Putting distance between me and her seemed to be the solution. It failed. The entire time I was in Japan, all I could think of was here. Who was she with? If she was seeing her old boyfriend. Or that guy from the party. Or both. I even thought of putting a tracker on her phone until I realized how insane that was. I was acting like a typical Morelli. Something I vowed to never do. I was not my brothers, I definitely was not my father. But that doubt, that jealousy, was still there in the back of my mind. During work, during rest, when I ate and when I slept.

"Is that what you were doing when I was away? Getting your business up and running?"

"I have to put that cool mil you gave me to use. What did you think I was up to?"

It was best not to tell her how wild my thoughts had gotten, even if she hadn't done anything. If she knew how I felt about her, she would use it against me. I could not let her have a weapon like that. Not a woman like her. "Shopping and stuff," I said.

"Right. Cause women be shopping." She looked hurt, and I almost wanted to take it back, but something in me, some protective spirit, made me double down. "It's not as if you've ever contributed to society before. You've only taken from it."

"And how have *you* contributed to society? From my perspective, you're the one who's stealing from people through both your legal and illegal businesses."

I stepped into her space. She did not step back like I thought she would and instead held firm and glowered back. Her eyes were glassy and her chin was shaking, but no tear fell. She was strong, I'll give her that. "You have no qualms spending the money I give you," I said.

Simona started and stopped, then started

again, straightening her posture as about to throw a retort, but then she backed down. She turned her gaze away from my face to the door. "Welcome home, husband. Now can you please get out of my way so I can do your bidding like I good little wife?"

"Good. Next time, hire a warehouse." I stepped out of her path and let her leave. I sighed as I leaned against the door, feeling all the strength leave my body. My eyes got heavy and my head ached. This wasn't the homecoming I intended. I didn't want to start a fight with her, but seeing her in her element triggered something inside me. She looked so carefree and focused and I was, I hate to say it, but I was warmed by it. Until I realized what I was feeling and for whom I was having those feelings. It was unfamiliar territory; one I was not used to being on and I had to get back to what I know.

What was worse is, it was the same feeling I had that time at the party. After we were done fucking, instead of going back to hatred and revulsion or even more indifference, I felt warmth. It was also the same feeling I felt when we had sex for the very first time five years ago. Nothing good came out of feeling like that. Only pain.

I listened as Simona told her people to leave, followed by shuffling of feet, rustling of paper, plastic, and fabric, then finally, silence. Mickey and Johnny were still there when I got out of the study. They were helping Simona clean the mess, and it seemed from the looks of it, they had neatly organized all the clothes on racks put in the corner. The two men looked at me apologetically, but I waved them off. It wasn't their fault this time.

I left them to their cleaning and went upstairs. When I finally descended back to eat, it was evening. I had asked my chef, a French man named Pierre, to whip up a meal for my return, and a mouth-watering aroma filled the dining room when I entered the dining room. Whatever he was cooking, it was worth the exorbitant amount I paid for him.

Simona was not in the dining room as I expected, but I didn't have to look for her. A trill of laughter drifted from the kitchen and filled the apartment. I followed the noise and found Simona and chef Pierre huddled over a pot of soup. One would think it was witches' brew in the pot the way they stared in wonderment, and then Simona laughed when it bubbled. Chef Pierre laughed as well. The man had been working for me for a few years now, but I have never seen him crack a smile. He was a no-nonsense chef who ruled his kitchen with the strictness of military dictatorship. But here he was, a man in his seventh decade acting like a schoolboy with crush. Then he invited her to taste the soup. She giggled. He smiled. They were comfortable with each other. One would think they've known each other for years.

"What's so funny?" I asked.

They both jumped when they saw me standing a few feet away from them. Chef Pierre's smile disappeared and his usual stern mask reappeared. His cheeks were red, but not from the heat. It was from being caught flirting with his boss's wife. Yes, you should be ashamed of yourself, fool. Simona, as always, was on a planet of her own. Her smile vanished when I took away her fun and she said, "Pierre was teaching me a recipe. Anything wrong with that?" Pierre interjected in a deep French accent. "Simona has been desperate for the recipe, so I was showing her."

"You two are on first name basis now?"

Simona replied, "Of course. When you were away, Chef Pierre would come and prepare food for us. He is your chef, isn't he?"

"Us?"

"Yes. Me, Johnny and Mickey."

"So you were a right little throuple while I was away."

"No. Chef Pierre would eat with us as well. It

felt odd for him to just cook and leave us." A foursome then. No wonder Mickey and Johnny were comfortably helping Simona like she was their sister. She only knew these men for a short while, but they were all having meals and god knows what else while I was away. "I hope he joins us for our dinner?" she said expectantly. Oblivious to the impropriety she's breeding among my stuff. No way was 'Pierre' eating with 'us'.

Chef Pierre was smart enough to jump in and offer an excuse about needing to check on his restaurant. He then told us to sit while he finished preparing the food, which he did in record time under my glare. The jovial atmosphere that was there before I came in was gone, and frankly, it was better this way. Simona, however, seemed genuinely sad to see her friend become distant. And when it was time for Pierre to leave, he got out, barely mumbling a goodbye. The apartment went silent after he was gone. The only sound that could be heard was the clinking of silverware against plates.

"You seemed very cozy with Chef Pierre."

She made a point to not look at me. Her attention was on her phone, which was beside her plate, and was scrolling on it when she spoke. "Like I said, we dined with him while you were away."

"He seemed smitten with you. Did you give him one of your famous blowjobs to turn an iron-hearted man like him into a marshmallow?"

She whipped up to face me. "He's old enough to be my father!"

"Has that ever stopped you before in your quest to seduce men to swindle? From what I heard, most of your victims were around his age."

"For your information the first time I—" she then shook her head and turned her attention back to her plate and her phone.

"What?"

"It doesn't matter. Believe what you want to believe."

"That you're a thief who seduces men before taking away their money? I don't have to believe that. I have first-hand evidence."

She dropped her spoon and sighed. Her head was still bowed when she said, "I didn't sleep with Pierre. Or Mickey. Or Johnny." When she looked up at me, there were tears in her eyes. "Will you always doubt me? Is this how you punish me?"

Had I pushed too far? Suddenly, I wanted to take away all my jibes and taunt and comfort her. The food in my mouth turned bland. Even the wine tasted like dyed water. Never have I been glad to be home and simultaneously wanted to be as far away from it as possible. "By the way," I said looking for a way to change the subject, "We've been invited to a wedding."

13

SIMONA

The wedding was a spectacular event. When Giovanni told me about his brother's wedding, I knew it would be grand. But entering the church and taking in the surroundings, it was clear that the bride and groom spared no expense. The cathedral was transformed into an oasis filled with white and pink blooms. The bride's wedding gown had a floral sweetheart bodice with ethereal lace embellishments that cascaded into a dreamy tulle skirt. She was the image of a beautiful bride. She looked happier than the last time I met her, which was, coincidentally, my wedding.

"Corina looks beautiful." I turned away from the blushing bride gliding down the aisle to Nico, who was practically speaking into my ear. I nodded. As the groom's closest relatives, they had placed together Nico and me in the front pew. It was just me and him in the pew, unfortunately. His other twin, Enrico, and his older brother, Gio, were acting as the groom's best men. "Why aren't you up there with the rest of them?" I asked. I would prefer he was there and not sitting next to me. Nico was quite talkative and had not shut his mouth since the ceremony started. Every other second, he would comment on every other thing. You could not tune him out. He would ask for my opinion on those things he was commenting on. From the church, to the priest and how he, Nico, used to be an altar boy at this very same parish. To the decorations which he thought were nice but too girly. Listening to him was so exhausting. I suspected it was Gio's plan to saddle me with his most talkative brother.

"Dante thought it would be better if I had little participation in the wedding. As if I would ruin his precious day." I wasn't surprised. Nico had a manic energy to him and anyone would be wise to keep him away from delicate events. "You looked better, though," he added. The bride had reached the front, and we all sat down.

"Huh?"

"As a bride."

I almost guffawed until I caught myself. The church was silent now and any sound would carry. He was being factitious or ludicrous. My wedding was closer to a shotgun wedding than this. The venue was arranged at the last minute and my dress was probably the first white thing the shopping assistant saw at the store. There was little thought to it. It had been serviceable, but that was about it. It was nothing compared to the custom-made designer dress Corina was wearing. "If you think lying will impress me, you're wrong," I said.

"I mean, she looks great and all, but you would have upstaged her. That's all I'm saying."

"Is that all? Or are you saying that because you brother iced you out?"

"No. Merely stating facts."

"If you think you're going to get an ally in me by trashing another woman, you thought wrong."

He rolled his eyes. "Ugh. You're no fun. I get why Gio likes you."

Again, I clamped down on another gurgle of

laughter. If only he knew what type of relationship his brother and I had. "Trust me, your brother doesn't like me," I whispered.

"Yeah, I know. You stole our family's money blah, blah, blah. But the way he's looking at you right now says otherwise."

I glanced up and saw Gio staring right back at us. His gaze had been on us the entire time, I see. It was the same intense gaze that had the power to turn up the heat inside me. I felt Nico's hand snake around my arm and he slid me towards him. I almost jumped at the sudden contact. "What are you doing?" Nico had a mischievous grin. "Just look at him," he whispered in my ear. To anyone else, it would seem like we were a couple talking intimately. And it no doubt looked like that to Gio. Knowing him and the accusations he made against me regarding Chef Pierre, he probably thought Nico and I were arranging a hookup later. Nico chuckled. "Man, I've never seen him this angry before. He looks like he's about to leap off from where he is and maul me off you." Abruptly, he let me go. "If you wanted proof, there it is. See, he likes you. He's never been able to shut up about you, ever since you two met."

"Only to curse me, probably."

"Yeah, but I could tell there was something

laden beneath those curses. Let's just say, I've never met anyone love hating someone as much as he did. I mean, he once told me that—" He glanced at Gio who was still glaring at us, and went silent.

"Told you what?"

Nico chose right this moment, after all his talkativeness, to shut up. He refused to elaborate further and asking the meaning of his statement only resulted in him giving me a cryptic look. The ceremony continued with no further conversation between us. I thought I could press him further, but by the time we got to the reception, a ballroom five minutes away from the church, he was gone. I had spotted him briefly with one of the bridesmaids, but even she, too, was nowhere to be found.

"Where's your brother?" I asked Gio when we settled down at our table. It was just the two of us so far, and the other chairs were empty.

"Which one?"

"Nico." Just I saw him pass us and called out to him, but he didn't respond.

"That's Rico, the other twin," Gio said. Of course. They both looked alike and were very hard to distinguish. "What do you want with Nico? I saw you two being rather cozy in church."

"You're going to have to ask him. He was the one being cozy with me."

"You have to be careful with Niccolo. He's not your typical mark."

"Ugh, not this again. I wasn't trying to fuck your brother. I wouldn't jeopardize the biggest source of money I've ever had by fraternizing with its employees and relatives, wouldn't I?"

"No. You're right," his mood shifted and in a low and serious tone he said, "I'm sorry for teasing you. And I'm sorry about the other night. I spoke to Chef Pierre, and what he described was at best a father-daughter relationship between you two."

I frowned. Where was this coming from? He was icy towards me ever since he came back from his work trip. He barely acknowledged my presence, and the only conversation we had was to tell me his brother had invited us to the wedding. Now he was being cordial? Something was up. "Nice to know you believe your employee over your own wife," I said.

"I'm trying to apologize." His voice was softer than my own accusatory one, which made me feel like a shrew, but I was too angry to care.

"Are you? Or were you embarrassed by your behavior the other night, especially after finding out you were completely off the mark? It sounds to me like you don't want to truly ask for forgiveness and just want to make yourself feel better. So you can go back on to your usual pedestal, where you look down on me."

He leaned back in his chair and crossed his arms. "That's a pretty portrait you've painted of me."

"Is it a lie? Sometimes," I shook my head as I realized that I've constantly wondered about this. "Sometimes, I wonder why you ever married me at all." It was obvious he hated me. He would not stop talking about it. And he seemed to not enjoy being married to me. The time we've spent together so far has been less than the time we spent apart. He was always on some trip or mission, and whenever we were together, we were rarely alone.

"I married you because I had to."

I smirked. "Nico says otherwise. Apparently, Dante was the one who was supposed to marry me. Nico told me you offered to do the deed."

"Niccolo likes to twist things. Dante already had someone he was in love with, as you can clearly see." He nodded his head towards the couple sitting at the high table as people came to congratulate them. They looked happy, and no one could doubt they were in love. Dante's hand would ever so gently wonder to Corina's from time to time and Corina would lean into him as if she was unconsciously gravitating to him. The last time I saw them there was a burning passion between them that did not seem to have simmered since. They were nothing like Gio and I.

"So you did it to save your brother from me. How noble."

"Is it so hard to imagine? Do we need to re-litigate how quick you lied and stole from me?"

When I couldn't come back with a similar retort, he leaned back in his chair with an air of smugness. I was tired of defending myself against someone who would believe nothing I said, so why bother? And besides, the twins and two bridesmaids joined us, so I couldn't say anything more, even if I wanted to. They were all coupled up. A coupling, I assumed that only happened at this wedding and will last the duration of said ceremony. Nico was now preoccupied with his date and would whisper some inane thing in her ear that would make her burst out laughing. Rico was similar. He and his date were also preoccupied with each other, leaving us the married couple acting like two strangers forced to share a table. The minutes seemed to last an eternity. With me pretending there was interesting stuff on my phone while Giovanni took some business calls. After a while, I sent a text to my mother to see how she was doing. She gained access to her phone at the center recently, and had been ringing me here and there. From the tone of her voice, she sounded happy, maybe a little chipper than I was used to, but it could be because of the lack of drugs.

"How are you doing?" My text said. She probably wasn't near her phone and I thought she would take some time to respond, yet a message appeared immediately. "Better than yesterday. And you?"

"I'm at a wedding. Dante's getting married." She sent three question marks. "Gio's brother," I responded. She took some time to send the next text which read, "does that mean you and Gio are getting along?"

Did it? My relationship with him was more fraught than ever and there hadn't been any progress happening. I would say it was regressing, but there was no way I was going to tell her that. The rehab center reported that her recovery was going smoothly, and a whiff of trouble might make her anxious. She felt guilty about my having to marry him after what happened, and I wasn't about to add to that guilt. "Yes," I replied. She sent a heart emoji, and I promptly felt a little better. Sometimes white lies were better than black truths.

The conversation moved to other mundane topics after that and just as I was about to reply to a question my mom asked, Nico leaned closer to me and asked. "What's going on between you two?" I put my phone away and turned to him. He had an elbow on the table and his chin in his palm, giving me an inquisitive glare.

"Me and who?"

He ignored my poor attempt at feigning ignorance. "You two have hardly talked the entire time you were together."

I motioned at the bridesmaid sitting beside him, who was currently typing on her phone. "Shouldn't you be minding your own relationship?"

"Don't try to deflect, I know you don't want to talk about my brother."

"You got me there. So let's get back to it. What did you mean earlier in the church?" Nico gave me a blank stare that had to be a put on. He knew what I was referring to. "You said Gio told you something about me. What did he tell you?"

A dawning realization came over his face, and a mischievous smile slowly spread. "I'm not sure if I should tell you." He glanced at Gio, who appeared too busy to care about our conversation. "He told me in confidence, after all."

"Fine." I opened the notes app and gave him

my phone. "Type it. That way, he won't know."

His smile got even broader. He didn't take too long. He typed what could be five characters and gave me my phone back. It was actually two characters he typed. Two emojis. A wedding ring and an infinity symbol. Try as I might, I could not work it out. Infinity meant forever. But the ring? Proposal? Marriage? Proposal forever? Married forever? That didn't seem like something he would type cryptically. He could have just told me. Or maybe… no. It could not be mean Gio wanted to propose to me all those years ago. No. Otherwise… no. It had meant something else.

"What do you—" When I looked up, Nico and his bridesmaid were gone.

14

GIOVANNI

"You don't look so happy. Is the idea of my getting married so repulsive?" I pulled away from my momentary reverie to see Dante staring back at me in the mirror as he was adjusting his collar. We were in his New York apartment, which was as light and airy as he was. Warm morning sun streamed through the windows and shined against the mirror, making it a little harder for me to see from my vantage point. I don't remember the room being this bright. Dante had a penchant for dark colors, so the new shades of yellow and blue were a surprise. A blue and white vase, yellow and white bedding. Even the drapes were a lighter color. Corina's influence had not just changed my brother's home, but his mood as well. He was something I never thought I would describe him as; giddy. I don't think I've ever seen him this happy ever since we were kids. He could not stop smiling. It was infectious. I plastered a smile of my own. "Yes it is," I said to him. "You getting married is like a gun shooting rainbows. It's sickly sweet and contradictory."

He chuckled. "It's Corina. Before her, the thought of marriage was suffocating. But now, I can't wait. I don't want to lose her again. Just thinking about..." his mood darkened and I knew where his thoughts had gone. To that night when he called me telling me Massimo had kidnapped Corina. Before that call, I thought Corina was like all the other women he had dated. I didn't think much about their relationship. He was usually distant with his women, and even when I saw him being a lot more affectionate with her, I thought he only cared for her. But when he called me, he sounded bleak. As if Saccone had snatched away his world from him. That was when I knew how much he loved her.

"It's over." I rubbed his shoulder. "No one is going to harm her again. They would have to come through me first."

He brightened and turned to me and said, "So what's marriage like? You're the only one of us who bit the bullet." He asked. I went to the chair with his jacket draped over and picked it up. "I don't think I'm the person to ask. My situation differs vastly from yours." I helped him put it on and brushed the few specks of lint off it.

"I never understood why you agreed to marry her, especially after what she did."

"Oh. You mean steal our money right when we needed it the most after tricking me into thinking she was the world's best pussy I had ever had?"

"Why does it sound like it's the last thing you hate her for more? And why do you make it sound so bad? I'm sure the twins would not have minded getting married to her. Although, she might have trouble with them than the other way."

"There was no way I was going to let her dig her claws into any of you."

"You sound like you're saving us from her."

"Funny. That's what she said."

"So, what do you guys do? I can't imagine you two constantly fighting each every day." His eyes glinted. "Have you done it yet?"

"What? Sex? Kinda had to, since her father was so adamant."

"About you two fucking? Ew."

"He's a bit… traditional. He thinks if the marriage is consummated we can't divorce."

Dante laughed.

I shook my head. Her father was fighting a losing battle. After we solidified our power, Simona was going to go. As much as I enjoyed her in bed, she was too much of toxic and erratic element to keep around. She was nothing but trouble and had caused a lot already in the few months we've been married. There was no way I was going to keep this going on for longer than a year. And a year was enough time for the family to be secure in its power. It was also enough time for me to get over whatever obsession I had developed for her. She didn't know this, of course. Watching her squirm at the thought of spending eternity with me was amusing.

"The father is weird I have to agree, but she seemed quite cool. Don't you think it's time you forgiven her?"

"If the same thing happened to you, would you forgive that person?"

Dante raised a brow. "You know, I get the reputation for ruthlessness, but I think you're way more ruthless than I am. I wonder what you have planned for her."

Fuck her. Get my revenge. Leave her on the

roadside. "My just desserts."

"Remind me to never get on your bad side. Come on," he tapped on my shoulder. "Let's go. I don't want to be late. Can you imagine if Corina arrived before I did?"

The ceremony went on without incident. Watching Dante being in love and being happy made me feel a little jealous. Corina fervently returned my brother's love. And he hers. I wondered what it was like to be with someone who loved you unconditionally and if I would ever experience it. And when that thought crossed my mind, my eyes searched for Simona in the crowd. She was sitting near the front next to my brother, looking beautiful and put together. She was like a porcelain doll. Cold. Beautiful. Emotionless. Looking for love from someone like her was like searching for water in a desert. You might find it, but odds are, it would be a mirage.

When the church ceremony ended and everyone was gathered at the reception, I told myself that I didn't want to be near her, but I was lying to myself. My heart lurched when a whiff of her scent tickled my nostrils, reminding me she was sitting next to me. I didn't want to. I strived not to, but my mind instantly went back to the last time I smelled that perfume of lilies and lavender on her neck. When I was ravaging her in the bathroom of some ballroom, not too dissimilar to the one we were now. My eyes instinctively sought out similar rooms in the ballroom. I spotted a powder room on the left, and several restrooms at the end of the hall. I could drag her into one of them and repeat what we did last time. Would she be willing? I turned to her. She was texting something on her phone. A boyfriend? The friend she met in Central Park Mickey and Johnny told me about? Whoever it was, the person on the other end of that conversation elicited a smile from her. I don't think she's ever smiled at me like that. I would love to — What was I thinking? Why should I care whether or not she was happy? My goal was not to make her life fun. My goal was to inflict misery, yet I was the one suffering. Fuck this. I thought. I wanted to some air.

Focusing on the activities wasn't helping. People were saying their speeches, and I had already said mine. I wanted to be away from her to clear my head, and Dante and his new bride were too happy with each other's company to want my gloomy mood to dampen theirs. The twins had found two bridesmaids who preoccupied them. I got up and went to look for a drink. A real one and not the lite shit being served. There was a bar just beyond the ballroom, partially empty. Only the bartender and two other patrons were there. I ordered a scotch, neat and chugged half of it down. This was better. My sour mood was already lightening as the alcohol softened my mind.

It was when I was nursing the rest of my drink that I noticed that the other patron who was at the bar counter kept glancing at me. I tried to ignore him at first, but after he glared at me for a solid five minutes, I finally turned to him and said, "What?"

He was a blond man, slender, and looked like he was in his twenties. He was dressed like every other guest in wedding clothes, but he didn't look like someone I would recognize. There was nothing about him that suggested he was part of Dante's crew. Quite the opposite. He reminded me of the carefree trust fund babies I had to deal with in my line of business.

"I'm sorry," he said, "It's just you looked so familiar and I didn't know how to open, but are you by any chance married to Simona M—"

Was he one of her ex-boyfriends? Or was it another mark? And why did all her men seem to pop out of nowhere everywhere I went? I thought of ignoring him and leaving the bar. My curiosity overshadowed my impatience for her shit. I nodded. "What's it to you," I added.

His face brightened at what I meant to be a cold and guarded response designed to brush off a person. "I knew I recognized you." He then took his drink in his hand, got off his seat, and came to sit on the stool next to mine. I guess social cues weren't his specialty. "You might not remember me, but I was at your home when you kicked us out." He extended his hand. "I'm Jack, Simona's assistant."

Something about him became familiar. I remember a man standing next to her noting things down when I came back home from a trip. I could not remember his face, but his height and build seemed similar to that man. If he was her assistant, it gave rise to more questions. "What are you doing here? Did she invite you?"

Jack withdrew the extended hand and adjusted himself in his seat. "No. Of course not. I came with a friend. She knows the bride. I didn't even know that it was the same Morelli family. Didn't even make the connection until I saw you."

I took a swig of my drink. "We are a small family."

He chuckled. "I don't know about that." Realizing the connotations of what he had just said, he blushed and cleared his throat. "Anyway, I was looking for Simona. Looks like I can't find her. Is she here? She's not answering my texts."

"Sounds like she doesn't want to be bothered."

He chuckled again. His laughter was more strained this time. Was I scaring him? Good. I hoped I was. He was irritating me and I wanted to drink my scotch in peace. "That's the thing. I think she would want to know about this."

I raised an eyebrow.

"Not that it's life or death or anything. It's just that…" he trailed off, and he looked unsure for a moment. "You know what, nevermind. I'm probably bothering you."

"Say what you want to say."

"It's just that — now I feel dumb for even bothering you about this. It's just that Simona has been using my storage space to store her clothes, but I need use of it now."

Storage? Clothes? "For her business?" I knew she had been looking for locations. Not that I was trailing her or anything, but my men had a tendency to give me the rundown of her activities without being asked, especially after the Leonardo debacle.

"Old clothes. You know, for her charity."

I almost choked on my drink. Simona has a charity? The woman had no generous bone in her body. Plus, I've never seen her doing any fundraising of any sort. If this poor man believed she had a charity, Simona likely deceived him.

Duped him into some scam or bilked him into storing her clothes without having to pay.

"Why didn't she look for her own storage space?" She had enough money to buy an entire warehouse if she wished to.

"Something about the logistics and storage spaces she couldn't use because of their location. I don't know. Will you be able to tell her? Because the need is a kind of urgent. My mother will be moving and she wanted to use it and I—"

"Sure," I said to cut off his long-winded and dreary explanation. "I'll pass on the message."

Jack bobbed his head and slid away. A few minutes later, he was out of the bar. I finished my drink and went to rejoin the rest of the group, my conversation with Jack still on my mind. Simona was alone at the table when I got back, looking pristine and perfect. How she kept herself perfectly put together always amazed me. I had an urge to muss up that perfection by untangling her hair, ruffling her dress, or kissing her. Or maybe all the above. Her gaze was on the people on the dance floor, radiating as she watched them dance, but as soon as it drifted towards me, she hastily wiped her smile away.

"What's so fascinating?" I asked when I was back in my seat.

"You know, you should have stayed where

ever you were. Things were so much fun when you weren't around."

"Sorry to darken the mood, but I had to act like the good husband at some point." I took her hand in mine and clasped it. "I don't think you would want news of me leaving you alone at my brother's wedding, spreading, no?"

Her gaze darted around the ballroom. Most people attended to their own affairs, yet a few gawked at us. Simona's relatives I assumed at first, but it might just as well have been people who liked to gossip. Our marriage was sudden, small and unexpected. And this was the first time were at a gathering where most families would have been invited. People would naturally be curious.

"So why did you leave me alone for an hour if you cared about talking?"

"Do you want me to leave and let the tongues wag? I could be all dramatic about it and give them a show."

She squeezed my hand tighter. "You better not do anything foolish."

"Don't worry. Besides, I met an interesting friend of yours. Or was it an employee who told me some interesting things?"

She let go of my hand and for a moment there, I almost wanted to grab it back. The contact of her hand to mine made my spine tingle that I should have gotten used to by now, but somehow I had not. Why was it always like this with her? A simple touch and my body was behaving like that of an eighteen-year-old.

"A friend of mine?"

"Some guy named Jack. He said something about a storage facility and some clothes you were keeping in there."

She took a deep breath and squirmed in her seat. Did I probe into something? She didn't look panicked, not yet at least, but she did not look comfortable. Maybe I should have engaged that Jack fellow further. "Um." She licked her lips and grabbed her phone. "Where did you see him? I mean, is he here?" She was frantically scrolling through her phone as she spoke.

"Came as a plus one with a friend, but why are you so worried? From what he said, it sounded like a simple logistics issue. Nothing is wrong, is it?"

She glanced up from her phone and squinted her eyes. "What did he say to you?"

"Something about you keeping your clothes there for charity, but I assume, of course, the charity part is a lie."

Like a switch, her frantic demeanor disappeared as she relaxed in her chair. Shouldn't she be panicking or did she realize how weak she looked and was now feigning strength? Then suddenly, she smiled. "Yes, the charity part is a lie. But I wouldn't have to go somewhere else if you didn't restrict my movements and where I was allowed to go."

"How am I a part of this?"

"You said I couldn't go downtown, remember? The place that has more and cheaper storage spaces. What was I supposed to do?"

For a minute, I had forgotten that Leonardo's family controlled that area. "How many clothes do you have that you need extra space than the closet at home?"

She shrugged. "Your apartment is fine, but a girl like me can never have enough."

"So you lie to get what you want?"

"I thought you said you knew me by now?"

"Yes. I know everything about you and it's ugly."

15

SIMONA

I don't know why I thought lying to him was a good idea. It was not. I should have just told him the truth, but I couldn't. I had a feeling that he wouldn't accept the truth, and that feeling turned out to be true. Gio was eager to believe the worst in me, that even when he was told the truth, he thought that was a lie. Although it pained me for him to have a negative perception of me, it was for the best. Turns out, a hate-filled Gio was easy to deal with. He was callous and mean, which meant he wasn't the heart-melting man I once knew, and that meant I wasn't in danger of falling in love with him again. Not with this brutal villain. This Gio was a constant reminder of how foolish I had been back in the day and I would not act like that again. I was smarter.

But not smart enough to resist him. In that department, he still had a hold over me. I only needed to point to the way I behaved when we came back from the wedding. I was angry at him; he seemed reviled by me, but the moment the doors to the penthouse closed and his lips clasped mine, I surrendered to him. To his rough and brutal lovemaking. I was with him all the way. From the moment he pressed me against the wall of the foyer and practically ripped my dress open. To the moment he dragged me down to the floor and fucked me like he was trying to exorcise a demon. It was quick, but no less arousing. I thought I was not going to come until the last moment when I screamed his name. Like all the other times I've had sex with him, my orgasm was bone melting. He always made sure I came before him. Not out of consideration of another partner, no. He made me come to prove he wasn't the only one under this awful spell. He wanted me and I wanted him. And we both hated that. Him just as much as I did. There was a toxic romance to it.

After we were done, I grabbed my clothes and rushed to my bedroom and opened the shower. I didn't want to sleep in his scent. I would only dream of him and Gio tormenting both my waking hours and my dreams were not something I wanted to go through. My shower was quick and soon I was done and ready to go to bed.

My sleep was dreamless and restless and I was up earlier than my usual time. There was no point in trying to get more sleep when I couldn't, so I got out of bed and went downstairs. Might as well make myself a cup of coffee, I thought. Say what you will about Giovanni, but the man had the best coffee machine in the world. The coffee beans themselves were even better. He had beans from every well-known coffee producing country. From Colombia to Kenya to Indonesia. It was like taking a trip around the world in a cupboard. I scooped a cup of the Jamaican blend and poured them in the steampunk-looking machine.

The apartment was quiet, making every sound echo such that when I heard the buzzer echoing, I jumped until I realized what it was. The lobby. I wasn't expecting guests, and Gio always mentioned if anyone would be coming up, including workers. But maybe he forgot?

"Hello?" I said into the intercom. Craig, the concierge cleared his throat. "Morning, Mrs. Morelli." His voice did not have its usual bored but assured tone. It quavered, and was high-pitched. "Uh, sorry to bother you so early in the morning, but there's a woman here who claims to know Mr. Morelli." In the distance, I could hear a soft voice say something inaudible to which the concierge responded with, "Of course." Then he said to me, "She says her name is Allison, and you might know her as well? She says she's been here before, but I don't recognize her."

Allison? We had spoken a few times since I met her, mostly via text and social media. We followed each other and she would like and comment on almost every post I made, even the inane ones. I hadn't seen her in person since.

"She knows Mr. Morelli?" I thought she was only my friend, unless it was a different Allison.

Just then, I heard the shuffling of footsteps descending the staircase. By the time I turned, was Gio strolling over to me. "Who is it?" he asked.

"A guest of yours, apparently. Allison?"

He paused and straightened his back. He seemed momentarily nonplussed, then he galvanized back into his regular self. "Give me the phone," he said.

I handed it to him and stepped aside. I was too

curious to leave, but I couldn't hear anything that was being said on the other side. Only Gio first talking in a commanding voice and asking the same question as I was, then his tone changed to soft as he said, "Hi. How are you doing? I didn't know you were in town." And then, "No, no, no, you're always welcome here." And finally, back to his commanding tone as he said, "Let her through," and hung up.

I waited for him to offer an explanation, but he didn't. Instead, he went to wait in the foyer next to the elevator. I followed him, my curiosity peaking higher and higher. "Expecting guests? You didn't tell me. I could have prepared," I said.

"I'm not." No elaboration. If he thought that would lessen my interest, he was mistaken.

"Allison. Huh? Who is she?" Is it the Allison I knew or a different Allison? I wondered.

"A friend."

"Huh. Didn't know you had any."

He never had time to respond. The elevator doors opened and Allison appeared. *That* Allison. The concern in the concierge's voice suddenly made sense. She looked like a drowned cat. Mud was splattered on her jeans, and her formerly white top, and her matted hair and mud-splattered face gave her a bedraggled look.

Giovanni immediately rushed to her. If he

thought of anything about her appearance, he didn't say.

"Hi." Her lips widened into a shaky smile. "I was in the neighborhood." She shrugged helplessly, her gaze squarely on Gio.

Gio took her hand in his and led her inside. "What happened?"

"A car sped into a pothole and lucky me got splashed. New York, am I right?" She glanced warily at me, but kept her attention on Gio. "It happened just as I was passing by your building," she said, "and I thought maybe I could borrow a shower and clean myself up?"

"It's fine. You can use the guest bathroom."

"Thanks. Sorry to bother you on a Sunday."

"Don't worry. You know where the bathroom is, right?"

She gave me a slight glance before going up the stairs. Gio's gaze was on her the entire time and even though he was standing with arms akimbo, there was a moment when he hesitated after she stumbled and almost fell. It was clear they had a history between them. His voice was tender when he spoke to her. I don't think I've ever heard him speak that softly to me now or ever.

A strange sense of dread settled over me as I pondered the implications of what this could mean. If she knew Gio, then she must have known me when we met, and if she did, why didn't she say anything then or since? It's not like I ever hid who I was. I literally brought her here that day I stumbled onto her in the park. Well, not here in this apartment, but in the lobby. Maybe she thought I lived in another part of the building? An innocent explanation for all of this was possible instead of the sinister track my mind was hurtling on.

"Who is she?" my voice came out strained, betraying my emotions. If Gio caught on, he didn't show it.

"A friend of mine."

"You said that earlier, but I don't think that's true."

He shrugged. "She's an ex who's now a friend."

"Is that all?" He sounded too casual as if trying to fool me. She was more than just some ex. I don't know why, but innate intuition was telling me she differed from the Russian lawyer ex we met at his friend's party.

"Why? Are you jealous?"

"Not at all. I was just wondering why you went all soft suddenly when you were interacting with her."

"Soft?" he frowned. Then brightened as his mouth widened into a smirk. "You're jealous of her, aren't you? Well, you don't have to worry, because unlike you, I intend to keep to our promise. And besides, she's only here to wash herself. Got any problem with that?"

"None. It's your home, after all."

"It's your home too."

"I don't know," I said. "It's just funny how the world works. She is my friend, too."

His brow furrowed. "What do you mean by that?"

"Allison and I are friends. Been friends for a while now too. We met a couple of months ago in Central Park. Johnny and Mickey can tell you all about it if you think I'm lying."

His puzzled expression would have been so fun to behold and I left him like that as I returned to the kitchen. The sudden presence of someone else in 'our home', as he liked to call it, made me forget I was in the middle of making the most delicious Sunday morning coffee. I grabbed my cup of already made, slowly turning warm coffee, and took a sip. It was still good to drink, so I sat down on one of the counter stools and watched Gio come in and make a cup of his own. I tried not to think too deeply about how he chose the same blend as the one I chose and instead let my mind wonder back to our new guest. She was either a creep or it was all coincidence. For now, I thought best to give her the benefit of doubt. "When did you date her?"

"Does it matter?" he said without turning to face me.

"I guess not. It's not like our relationship is like any normal one. I mean, who cares who you or I fucked before we met, right?"

His jaw clenched and his body stiffened a little before saying, "It was before I met you."

"Oooh. So, you were getting over a breakup."

"And after."

That pang returned. It was deeper and strained at my heart much longer. "An on and off girlfriend. Sounds like you two were serious."

He faced me and looked like he was about to say something, but his gaze then lifted from my face to an object beyond me. "You're done already," he said in that same soft tone that was irritating me more and more for no real reason.

"This is the only thing I could find." Behind me, Allison was standing barefoot in a white terry-cloth robe, her hair damp.

"I think Simona can help you with some clothes."

"Huh?" The thought of her wearing my clothes made my skin crawl. It shouldn't. It was irrational but nothing was making sense so far and Gio did not see any problems with it. He raised his eyebrows and added, "You have so many clothes, after all."

"I do," I replied. "That's true, but I doubt your friend would want to wear my clothes."

Allison agreed with me. "Yeah… I don't know. I can just throw my clothes in the washer and wear this while my stuff is getting cleaned."

I was with her until that last part. The thought of seeing her parading in this place with nothing but a robe on was unsettling. It was clear from how Giovanni behaved that there was more going on between them than Allison simply being an ex.

"I have something else she could wear. There are some new clothes that came in last week from the shop that had minor defects. Some sweats and a tank top. Unworn. I could give you those?"

She gave me a sweet and heartwarming smile. Her eyes were still weary and apologetic and it made me feel guilty for being hurt or jealous. "That would be great," she said. I got up from my chair, made my way to the little room I had turned into a storeroom for the clothes we had rejected. These clothes, including the ones in my assistant's storage room, we're going to go to our charity, so I might as well give them to someone in need.

As I went through the racks looking for the

most appropriate and right sizes, I thought it was funny that Gio thought these were mine. If he even cared to investigate before accusing me of hording clothes, he would see what a ridiculous notion that was. The clothes were of different sizes for starters and there were more than one of the same style. Whatever. He would probably come up with something else to accuse me of, anyway. I was never, or will I ever be, a good person in his eyes. Suddenly feeling frustrated, I eventually grabbed a pair of sweats I thought she would fit and a tank top.

Allison and Giovanni were deep in conversation when I came back. They had moved to the living room and were casually sitting on the couch with cups of coffee in hand. Their conversation wasn't awkward or stilted like one would expect a conversation between two exes would be like. They were like old friends who hadn't talked recently and were eager to catch up. Gio seemed enraptured by whatever Allison was currently talking about. It sounded inane to me. Something about a bird she saw in South America. When the story ended, he responded with a long 'wow.' I wanted to roll my eyes. One would think she was talking about saving the Amazon the way he looked so enraptured. They were both so wrapped in their conversation, they didn't notice me entering the room.

Allison slowly leaned forward, and her robe parted slightly, revealing a glimpse of her cleavage. Gio's gaze followed the movement, as did mine. I was sure the robe wasn't that loose when I left. A sudden urge to grab her and hurl her out of the window came over me. Maybe claw her eyes out first. It was an irrational feeling that took me a minute to clamp down. I wasn't going to do anything close to that. No, I'm a better person than that, but I wasn't going to let her stay in that robe longer than necessary.

"I found this. Don't know if it will fit, but they look to be your size." My voice cut through their talk and they both turned to face me. Allison and Gio looked like a well-matched couple. Her pale, Nordic-like skin complemented his Mediterranean olive. She was a tall blonde beauty and he was a tall handsome man. An Icelandic model and her Italian billionaire boyfriend. Allison looked like she belonged here and made me feel like an intruder by her mere presence. What was up with me? I was better than this. She put her coffee cup down, got up and glided towards me before taking the sweats and t-shirt.

Allison unfurled the sweats and said, "They look good." She took the clothes but didn't do anything else. She just stared at me with a slight smile that was almost a smirk. It could not have been a smirk, could it? A moment of awkwardness passed between us, after which I let out a nervous chuckle. "What?" I said.

"Nothing," she replied. "It's just that," she glanced at Gio and then back at me and said, "I didn't know you two were a thing… When we bumped into each other and you took me here, I never made the connection…"

"It's fine," I said. "It's a small world."

"Right," she said, "Of course. If I had known that I was actually befriending my ex-boyfriend's current girlfriend…" she trailed off again.

"Oh. Gio and I are married," I said. I was sure she knew this, but maybe the information slipped her mind. And if she was acting surprised, she was a brilliant actor because her eyes widened as they darted between Gio and me, then she said, "Oh, my god! When!"

"Happened while you were in Brazil," Gio said.

Allison's mask slipped a little, and I was sure I saw worry on her face before it went back up again. She beamed, a little too much if you were to ask me, and said in a cheery voice, "Congratulations. Must have been love at first sight."

"It was, uh—" While Gio was scrambling for something to say, I jumped in. "What can I say?

He swept me off my feet and a few months later, we were married. How could I say no to such a handsome man?"

"Wow," Allison said. Even when she spoke, her voice didn't sound convincing. "I never thought he would do it. I've always seen Gio as a perpetual bachelor. Never to be tied down by anyone."

"He must have been waiting for the right woman to come along." I was going to end my statement there, but then I saw Gio's clenched jaw and realized he did not like any of what I was saying. Good. I added. "He must love me that much."

"Right. Yeah." Her gaze darted between me and Gio before awkwardly saying, "I'm going to go put this on and see if I can fit."

She went upstairs again, leaving Gio and me alone. Immediately after I heard the guest bedroom door close, Gio said, "In love?"

"Did I do anything wrong? I simply said what I should say as per our agreement. Appear like we love each other to the public and all that bullshit?"

He narrowed his eyes.

"Funny you're angry because I think I'm the one who deserves that, right? I wasn't the one flirting with my ex-girlfriend."

"You sound jealous."

"I'm just let you know you should keep to the agreement you came up with."

"Is that right?"

"Did I say anything wrong?"

"I don't know. It's just I've never seen you this riled up." He folded his arms and leaned back. "You're intimidated by her."

"Me? By some supermodel who spent her time in South America doing some inane shit? No."

He chuckled. "The inane shit she was doing was an environmental project to save an endangered bird in the Amazon rain-forest. I don't know what you heard, but she's not like you."

I rolled my eyes. Of course, she was not only beautiful, she also had a heart of gold and saved birds during her spare time. "If she's so amazing, you should have married her."

He leaned in and stared me directly in the eye. "If your father wasn't such an extortionist, maybe I would have."

I gazed into his eyes to see if he was being truthful, but I could not detect deception. My suspicions were correct, but I didn't expect that she was that important to him. "You wanted to marry her?" I asked.

I never got my answer. Before he could say anything, I heard a sound at the top of the stairs and saw Allison coming down. How long was she standing there? I wondered?

16

GIOVANNI

The question hung in the air like a foul smell. There was a time I thought I wanted to marry Allison. We got on well. She was the first woman I truly cared for. Contrary to popular belief, I have a heart in there somewhere and it felt something for Allison. Had it been love? No, probably not. But she was someone I got along with and would have been a suitable candidate for the mother of my children. I never felt that heart-stopping, violent affection for her, but I liked her. She was stable, predictable, and calm. But I didn't propose and strangely enough, I don't feel regret.

One would think someone in a horrible marriage such as myself would be yearning for a different wife, but that was not how I felt when I saw Allison for the first time in a long while. She was still the same person, still beautiful, still charming, but whatever fire that burned for her before was now extinguished. We were friends who had kept in touch over the years. Simona seemed to think we were more than that. And I didn't know if I wanted to disabuse her of that notion. Seeing Simona getting jealous was validating. My toxic heart couldn't get enough of it. It was more evidence that she and I were in the same boat. We hated each other, but we still wanted each other. If only physically.

Before I could answer Simona's question, I heard a throat clearing. Allison was standing at the foot of the stairs wearing the clothes Simona had given her. They were over-sized and plain, but Allison could wear them like haute couture. She had a knack for making any article of clothing look good on her. It's probably why she initially turned to modeling before focusing on environmental issues.

"I think I'll be going back now," Allison said. If she had heard what Simona and I had been saying before, she didn't give any sign.

"You don't have to leave now," I said. It was more out of courtesy, but she also looked like she needed it. She looked gaunter than I remembered. And besides, we hadn't caught up in a while and I genuinely enjoyed her company. "We were about to have breakfast," I said. "Join us."

Allison twiddled with her thumbs. "I don't want to intrude."

"You won't be," Simona said. "I was on my way out. You two can enjoy catching up or whatever."

"You're leaving?" Suddenly, I didn't want Simona to leave. "Where to on a Sunday?"

"Contrary to popular belief, Gio, I don't enjoy inconveniencing people." She must have read my confusion because she then said, "I'm meeting Jack and taking the clothes out of his hands. And maybe look for a new place to store them while I'm at it."

I wasn't sure if this was one of her ploys and if it was, I couldn't tell to what end it could be. She seemed like she genuinely would rather be elsewhere, even though a few minutes ago she looked like it was Allison she wanted to push out.

"I should call Mickey." Maybe he could not

only keep her safe, but prevent her from doing something ridiculous.

She waved her phone. "Already did, and he'll be here in five."

"Good."

As Simona strolled past me, I took hold of her hand and drew her to me so I could place what I initially intended to be a perfunctory kiss on her lips. Her lips were so soft and inviting. Brushing against them lightly was temptation enough for me to coax open her lips and kiss her deeper than I intended. Her tongue played with mine, wrecking my insides. When I let go of her, I realized I might have taken it farther than I had initially planned on. It was supposed to be a simple kiss for Allison's benefit and for us to keep up our ruse, but it almost spiraled into me taking Simona onto the couch and fucking her in front of Allison. Even Simona looked surprised. If she thought she had an upper hand, I wiped that thought away from her head, whispering into her ear, "Don't do anything foolish. That was a reminder of who you belong to."

"Shouldn't I be saying the same about you," she said, then yanked her hand away and made her way to her room. A few minutes later, she was out of the apartment.

"So it is true," Allison said after we were alone.

"What is?"

"You and Simona being in love. To be fair, I have to say I wasn't convinced, but the way you look at her. It says everything."

"How do you two know each other?" I asked.

"She bumped into me while I was cycling in the park," Allison said. "I had no idea who she was until now. But I won't let you avoid the topic."

"I don't think I was doing any such thing."

She laughed. "It's fine to admit that you're in love with your wife, you know. That's the normal thing."

"Am I that obvious?"

"It's impossible not to notice," she said smiling, "Whenever she's in the room, she's the only person you see. Your gaze follows her every move. It's quite cute, actually. Who would have thought it? Giovanni Morelli is in love."

"Things change. People change," I said. I should be glad that our ruse was working even on someone like Allison, a friend of mine, but I still felt guilty for not telling her the truth.

Allison tilted her head to the side. "I don't know. I would have bet a million dollars that you would remain the same."

"That's an odd insult."

"It's a compliment. You are constant. Not

predictable, but constant nonetheless." She glided over to the sofas and plopped herself onto one. "So, what made you change? What's so special about Simona?"

I tried to think of what to say. Toss in a few lies about how she was the most amazing person in the world, something sappy like that. But Allison would sniff it out. She knew me long enough. The truth is better. "Simona is a box of surprises. You never know what she's doing next, or what you'll find out about her. She keeps me on my toes."

"You make her sound like she's suspect and you're a detective trying to catch her."

"I'm happy, if that's your concern."

Allison shrugged. "I can't argue with that." It was as if my response was not what she wanted to hear. I'm not sure if I was mistaken or not, but I thought I saw her face grimace when I spoke about Simona positively, but that's could have been a trick of the light. Allison was the last person I could ever suspect of jealousy. She was comfortable talking about exes. She differed from Simona in that regard. I should prefer her attitude to Simona's but somehow, I got a kick out of Simona's jealousy. It meant she felt something for me, however little.

We were soon interrupted by my maid, Brita,

whom I gave instructions to clean and iron Allison's clothes. After that, I offered Allison breakfast, which she declined. She said something about being on some sort of fasting diet. So we drank coffee while her clothes were being prepared. Brita came back with a neat stack of ironed clothes in her hand and presented them to Allison.

"That was quick!" Allison said. She sounded disappointed. Maybe she had been enjoying our conversation and wanted to stay longer, I thought. There wasn't any harm in her being around for a few more hours. We were just friends.

"You don't have to go," I replied.

"I don't know about that," Allison replied whilst taking the clothes from Brita. "Your wife might rip me to shreds if she comes back and finds me here."

So Allison, too, had noticed Simona's reaction. I wanted to tell her it had more to do with Simona's mistrust of me, and I couldn't exactly tell her that without telling her the truth about my marriage. Instead I said, "We had a long day yesterday. That's probably why she seemed grumpy. She has no taste for blood."

Allison chuckled. "You'd be surprised. I know a lot of women who do anything in their power to keep a threat away from their man." Gesturing to her clothes, she said, "I better get dressed."

Half an hour later, she was gone. With nothing else to do, I went to my study and got to work. Concentrating was hard. The more time passed, the more I wondered where my wife could be. I didn't want to be a weirdo stalker prick and call her to find out where she was. She had already told me, after all. But my mind went to that dark place again and again. Where Simona and that assistant of hers were not only colleagues but lovers. Images of her and him fucking in a storage tormented me until finally when it was late in the afternoon, I gave up and dialed her number. It rang for so long I thought she would never answer. She picked up on the last ring. "What now?"

She sounded irritated. It only made me irritable in turn. "Where are you?"

"Why do you care? I thought you and Allison were catching up like old pals."

"Are you going to answer your question?"

She sighed and said, "I'm on my way back, not that I should tell you."

"Good." I ended the call. I shouldn't be excited by the news, but I was. The place felt lonely without her, as much as I hated to admit it. Another thing I didn't want to admit was my eagerness to see her back in my home. It was odd, this hate I had for her. It made me want to throttle and make love to her simultaneously.

She was lying when she said she was on her way. It was evening when she came back. By then I had gone from anxious to angry, to anxious to angry again.

"Where were you?" I asked when she returned.

She rolled her eyes in a way that made me wanted to shake away her insolence and kiss her until she was moaning my name. "Not this again."

"What did I say? I only asked a question."

"Am I going to get a Guantanamo level interrogation every time I come back a little late? If you're so worried about where I was, why don't you ask your man?"

She was right. Somehow, I ended up being more aggressive than I had originally planned on, making me look like the obsessed husband I despised. Thing is, she looked weary and the hem of her jeans were tipped with dust. I genuinely wanted to know what she had been up to all day, but asking any more wouldn't come out well, so I dropped the subject.

"I was preparing dinner," I said.

She raised her eyebrows and her gaze went to the kitchen towel on my shoulder as if noticing it for the first time. She scoffed. "You? Cooking."

"It's a reconciliatory dinner."

"Oh. That's new. Did Allison put you up to it?"

It was something I had been thinking about after Allison left. Her presence jolted me to the realization that I was tiring of the constant fighting and bickering Simona and I were engaging in. It made us mistrust one another, and if we were going to be in this marriage thing for longer than three months, trust was important.

"Allison left soon after you did. And that's another reason for the dinner."

"I have no interest in discussing your old flames with you, Giovanni."

"I don't mean it like that. Can you at least agree to the dinner? It's mushroom risotto. Your favorite."

Her eyes narrowed. "How did you know that?"

"Contrary to popular opinion, I actually listened when you told me what your favorite food was."

"Flinging my words back at me. Nice tactic."

I raised my hands in mock surrender. "It's not. Genuine honesty coming from yours truly."

She seemed to mull it over in her head and then her shoulders slumped and she said, "Fine. I need to take a shower first. I'll be down in a few."

"Good."

I had Brita help me set up a candlelit dinner outside on the terrace. It was a beautiful warm summer night with the backdrop of the city skyline. When Simona came out, she looked around at the setup with slight amusement. "If had known it was going to be grand, I would have worn a dress." I quickly placed the risotto dish on the table and glanced at her. She had removed her jeans and was wearing cute shorts that showed off her shapely legs and a top that clung to her breasts.

"You'll do," I said, "Take a seat. Dinner is served."

I went to my chair, and she sank into the only other chair. The candles made her face glow, inducing an angelic vibe to her. Her beauty was striking. It caught one off guard, even one who had seen her multiple times like me. I might have stared for too long because she tilted her head slightly and furrowed her brow. I shook my head and scrambled for something to say. "You look better in simple shorts and a tank top, than dolled up and in heels, by the way."

"Thanks, I'll remember to wear this to the next formal event we go to."

"That would definitely grab attention," I said.

"And you'd like that, wouldn't you? Me getting laughed off for being both a clown and a whore."

"Simona."

"Did I lie?"

"I want us…" We had been fighting for so long I didn't even know how we could be amicable to each other. I had to tread carefully. It was going to be difficult for her to believe that this was real. "I want us to be amicable."

She smirked.

"It's the truth."

"Why is it I find it hard to believe you?" There was a spark in her eye that showed she was at least willing to hear me out. It made me press on.

"You're right. You have no right to believe anything I say, but aren't you tired? I know I am."

She leaned back in her chair and looked as if she was assessing me to see if I was telling the truth. I could hear the gears in her head turning, wondering if this was some sort of play. "Did your ex put you to this? Was it her suggestion?"

"Allison has no idea what our relationship is

like. And it's not like she was here long enough. She left soon after you did."

Simona shifted in her chair. She glanced down at the food as if for the first time and placed some risotto on her plate. "So you didn't fuck her while I was gone?" she said in a low voice.

"I would never fuck anyone who's not you here."

"Really? Even after we divorce?"

"If that's what you want, you can put it in the settlement."

"Okay. What's the play here?" she said. "Is there some new contract I'm not aware of? Did my father contact you?"

"No."

Her eyes narrowed, assessing me again for what felt like the nth time. Finally, she said, "You're right. I'm tired of us fighting. I'll agree to your terms of the truce under one condition."

"Which is?" I was nervous. What if she had played me instead?

"You come to my store opening."

"That's it?"

"I know it's not on the scale of some of the things you get to do, but it's important to me. My employees were surprised to see you when you came in last time. Most of them probably thought I wasn't married."

"So you want to use me as what, arm candy to your friends?"

"Would it be so bad if the shoe is on the other foot this time?"

"Fine. You've attended my stuff. It's only fitting that I come to yours."

"Great. So how do we sign the truce? With a kiss?"

"If you prefer." I knew she was being sarcastic, but my invitation was more honest.

"Let's eat first," she said. "I'm dying to know how good you are at cooking." She took a forkful into her mouth. I watched her as she chewed and wondered why I was feeling anxious. It could not be because I wanted her approval.

"Better than I expected," she said after a few chews.

"Great. Because that and an egg are the only things I can cook."

Her laugher filled the night air. "Why risotto? I would have thought you'd have learned a simpler dish like boiling noodles."

"I can do that as well. But I liked it so much when I was a kid, I would beg my mom to make it every day. One day she tired of my begging and taught me to cook."

"So we share a favorite dish. Interesting. That's one area we're compatible."

"We're compatible in other areas as well."

She blushed and took a sip of wine. "You never told me about your mother."

As much as I aspired to be on good terms with Simona. Trading stories about our parents was one area I didn't want to go to. Especially when it came to my mother. "She was an exceptional woman," I said, hoping to end the conversation.

"And an artist," she said. Simona must have noticed my discomfort and my unwillingness to go there. My mother was a topic I rarely broached with friends, let alone the women I slept with. But she was different, wasn't she? She was my wife, and I had just agreed to be cordial with her.

"She loved to paint. My mother would spend hours on end in her studio painting all day. The tips of her fingers were practically black with paint."

Simona smiled. It looked genuine. "She sounds very passionate."

"She was. And it's not like she wasn't attentive to her children or anything. I spent more days with her when she was alive than I did with my father."

"You were her favorite?"

"That's what my brothers would say, but I don't agree. I just came whenever she called."

She bellowed again. Her laughter was so infectious, I chuckled. Our talk moved on to other topics, which I was glad of. We had more in common than I thought. It was odd that I found her talk of fashion interesting, but I did. I could listen to her all day. Hell, maybe I could listen to her read the phone book all day. I wasn't sure if it was her topics I found interesting, or her. This moment brought back memories. Back to a time when I thought our relationship could be different. Maybe…

My phone rang, breaking into the cocoon we had created.

"Pick it up. It's okay," Simona said. I would rather let it go to voicemail. Our time together was enjoyable for the first time in our marriage, and I didn't want to ruin it by taking a business call. I checked to see who it was. It was Allison. I answered the phone.

17

SIMONA

I was going to leave him. I had a plan before I entered the apartment. Before he could do or say anything, I was going to tell him I decided to move out and find a place of my own. It made sense in my mind. I was tired of constantly fighting. And I was sure we had convinced anyone important that our marriage was real, so there was no longer any need for us to keep up the ruse. But what really pushed me was Allison. It was clear Giovanni harbored some feelings for her, try as he might to deny it. After my initial wave of jealousy had dissipated, I could tell that he and Allison had a connection. He seemed happy to see her. He even smiled. I don't think Gio has ever smiled at anything I've ever said or done and that made me realize how unhappy our marriage was. Even my assistant had noticed the tiredness behind my eyes wasn't just from the store opening, but something else. He was too kind to mention anything more than, 'how's your day' though. He was smart enough to recognize that I didn't want to talk about it.

So when Gio asked me to join him for dinner, I was surprised. When he suggested we stop fighting, I was suspicious. He had shown no inclination towards a truce before and I was sure it was some sort of ruse whose purpose I hadn't worked out yet. But as the dinner went on, I felt like he was genuine. We spoke cordially for the first time in probably years. There was even a point when he was talking about his mother that made me think he was opening up. Then the call happened.

Apparently, Allison was downstairs and was distressed. When she came up, she looked even more disheveled than she did earlier in the day. Her clothes, which I had given her earlier, had torn in places. Her shoes did not match what she had on, something that stuck out to me. As if she had grabbed the first pair in her closet and got out. The mascara on her face was runny from crying and her eye was purple and puffy. Something had gone horribly wrong. An awful pun came to mind; she had a knack for dramatic entrances.

"What happened?" Giovanni asked, rushing over to her.

"I left him," she said. "I left Carter." Her voice was shaky. She sounded like she was going to break into sobs any minute, but she didn't. "I couldn't take it anymore. I just ran out."

Gio embraced her into a tight hug, and she wailed into his chest. "Okay. It's okay." He held her for a while and when she calmed down, he led her slowly to the living room. I followed behind, feeling a little out of sorts. Who the hell was Carter? "Sit down and tell us everything," Gio said as he pressed her gently down on the couch. He sat next to her while I sat opposite them. Allison took a deep breath and went into her tale. According to her, she had a boyfriend she was living with. Carter, who, from the sounds of it, was an abusive drunk. They had an argument after he saw her wearing different clothes than the one she went out wearing. Carter tore at them during the fight, then he punched her. She then decided it was too much and left. My jaw was open as I listened to her story. I felt guilty for ever thinking negatively about her. Clearly, she was going through a lot.

"I didn't think. I just ran. I grabbed a few things and got out with no clear thought. Your apartment was the first place that came to mind and that's how I ended up here. I'm so sorry if…" A gust of wind blew through the open French doors and Allison looked outside. "Oh, did I ruin your romantic dinner? I'm so sorry."

"It's fine," I said to her. "We were already done, anyway."

"I'm so afraid to go back to that place," she said, and I completely understood her. Who knew what else her boyfriend would do if she went back? "You can stay here for the night," I said.

She smiled. "I won't be intruding? I just thought I would get here and then maybe book a hotel and stay—"

"There's absolutely no need for you to stay at a hotel. Right Gio."

Gio nodded. "We have more than enough room," he said.

"I don't want to intrude," Allison said.

"You wouldn't be," I cut in. "You said you took some things with you. Are they in the lobby?"

"Yes. My suitcase. Honestly, I just threw stuff in there. I wasn't even thinking straight."

"I'll tell Craig to bring it up," Gio said.

While he went to do that, I led Allison to the downstairs bathroom where a first aid kit was available and helped to her dress her wounds. She had a few scratches on her hands besides the purple eye that was quickly turning puffy. "Did you go to the police?" I asked her. "Maybe get a restraining order?"

She smiled, and it quickly faltered. "Already had a restraining order on him, but he ignored it and when I threatened to call the police," she pointed to her eye, "this was the result. I don't think I can deal with all the rigmarole of going through the system. Carter can be slippery."

"Maybe Gio can help."

"He's already helping enough letting me stay here. And I doubt Carter will have the balls to come after me once he knows I'm under the protection of the Morelli family."

I dabbed her face with a cool cloth to ease the redness of her eye. She looked so vulnerable in this state it was impossible not to feel sorry for her. I wondered if that was why she had initially come here early on. She might have intended to leave her boyfriend and come here, but was taken aback when she saw me. No wonder she acted the way she had. "This Carter guy sounds like a piece of shit," I said. She chuckled softly and winced, touching her temple.

"I'm sorry," she said.

"About what?"

"Not telling you about my relationship with Gio." She cast her gaze away from me and went into a rambling explanation. "It's just that when you invited me back here the first time, I thought it best not to mention it, thinking we would only meet each other once and that would be it. And then we became sort of friends, and the more we got closer, the harder it became to say something."

"I get it. You think you should say something, but you don't and then things spiral and suddenly it's too late. But maybe a heads up would have been great," I said.

"Next time."

We both laughed.

After I finished dressing her wounds, I led her out of the bathroom where Gio was waiting for us. He looked a little surprised when he saw us coming out smiling. What was going through his head? I can only wonder. I would like to think he thought we were talking about him and he was anxiously wondering what we had said.

"I've prepared a room for you if want to go to

bed," he said to Allison.

"That would be nice," she replied. Gio took her into his arms and led her upstairs. He must have put her in the other guest room, I thought as I went back to the balcony. The food had gone cold and I no longer had an appetite, so I gathered it and sent it to the kitchen. I went about putting all the leftovers in the fridge and making a mental note to take some to work for lunch. And make sure Gio wouldn't notice me packing it. Knowing I liked his food that much might make him go insane, actually. After I was done putting away everything and hiding away a lunch box behind some bottles of water, I closed the fridge only to encounter Gio's big body right beside me. Latent adrenaline made me jump and squeal, causing Gio to chuckle.

"What were you up to in there?"

Did he see me packing away the lunch and hiding it away? It would be mortifying if he had been watching me the entire time. But no. I would have sensed him if he had been in the kitchen for long. Like it or not, every time he entered my radius, the hairs at the back of my neck would rise and my heart would pound just a little louder, just as it was doing now. And the little smirk he had on was not helping matters. To wipe it away and gain some equal footing, I slapped his shoulder. "You scared me," I said.

That only made his smile widen. "Where you up to no good?"

"If putting away dinner and cleaning up is being up to no good, then yes."

He raised his eyebrows.

"What? Surprised I can clean after myself."

He must have realized how his reaction must have seemed to me because his mood changed and became serious. "Thank you."

"Well, I ate the food too, and you cooked. The least I could do is clean."

"I mean for what you did for Allison and letting her stay here."

"It's not like it's my place. You have more say on who stays here than I do."

"Well, you're my wife. What's mine is yours." I don't think he meant it literally. It sounded like a throwaway phrase, but part of me couldn't help interpreting it as something more meaningful. The way he was looking at me was also not making it any clearer. He stared into my eyes as if I was the only person in the world. It was unsettling. It made me want to jump to any other topic that wasn't us.

"Is she asleep?" I asked.

"Probably. She looked a little tired, but I gave her a sleeping pill, regardless. She needs to rest."

I nodded. The best thing for Allison right now was to get some rest. I could not imagine what she was going through right now.

"Which brings me to another subject," Gio said. "You're sleeping in my room."

"Why," I said in a light tone, "are all the rooms taken? I'm fine in my room." This place had four bedrooms. There was more than enough space for three people to sleep in.

"Not when there's another person around. We can't keep up the happily married ruse with us sleeping in different bedrooms."

"But I like mine!" I could feel the tone of my voice rise in panic. Even though we've slept together a few times now, we've never done it in bed and the thought of being under the same sheets as his made my temperature rise. Lately, I've been having dreams of him sleeping naked and me joining him, but before anything happens, I would wake up. I couldn't sleep in the same bed as him and have those dreams. What would happen? I might maul him in my sleep. No. It would not do. "I can't sleep with you," I said.

"The bed is big enough. We can both fit." He was taunting me. The laughter in his voice was an indicator. Was he serious? His eyes said he was, and it didn't look like he was going to let up any time now. "I can't sleep with you in the same bed."

"Why not? It's not like we haven't fucked before." He put emphasis on the word 'fucked' that it was easy for my brain to conjure up images of all the times we had done so. The way his body felt against mine. His hot skin rubbing against mine. How he enveloped —

"Don't care. We're not sleeping in the same bed." It clicked then that I've never been in his room before. "Doesn't your room have a couch or something? You can sleep there? Or I could, if you're so fond of your bed."

"It doesn't. It has two somewhat comfortable chairs, but not good enough to sleep in. They're great for other things though," he said. I rolled my eyes at the double meaning. Try as I might, it seemed like there was no way out. He was right about us sleeping in the same room. It made sense and it would be difficult to explain to Allison why we were in separate rooms and I couldn't think of a plausible excuse myself. "Fine," I said. "We sleep in the same bed, but no funny business."

He guffawed. "You sound like my eighth-grade schoolteacher." Raising his hands, he added, "I'll make sure to leave enough space for Jesus."

Anyone who doubted our ruse would look at his room and have those doubts confirmed. There was no hint of femininity here. It was a lot of dark colors intermixed with pale blue and white. It was the bedroom of a bachelor, not a man married to a woman. But maybe our whirlwind romance and quick wedding cover story would be good enough of an explanation. I looked around and at anything but the bed, feeling a little out of sorts. It was as if I had entered his private space, but not as an equal but as a naïve prey led into the lair of a predator.

"You should bring some of your things in here. At least while Allison is around. I figure she might stay for a few days, maybe a week," Gio said as he strode past me and went into a room beyond which I assume was the bathroom. A week? Of course, she would stay here for a couple of days or more. Somehow I had thought she would leave tomorrow and all of this was only for tonight, but if she was staying for a week, that meant Gio and I had to sleep together for the same amount of time! Could I handle Gio's body inches away from mine?

I stared at the bed, giving it my full attention for the first time. How many women had had the pleasure of being brought to ecstasy on that bed? A wave of jealousy stronger than any I've ever felt tugged at me as images of women having sex with Gio rotated in my head. He was a known playboy. He must have had gone through half the women in this city. I closed my eyes and shook my head to dispel the images, but one remained. That of me and him tangled in those sheets. It was both hot and scary. I tried to dispel that too, but it remained at the back of my mind. My own special taunt played by my mind.

Instead of standing in the same spot dumbstruck, I galvanized into action and went to my room, where I gathered a few of my things and put on pajamas. Nightdresses were out until further notice. When I came back, Gio was already sitting in bed reading a book. The image would have been nerdy and domestic if weren't for him being in just his trunks.

"You're half naked!" I said.

"And you've dressed for the Siberian winter. What's with pjs Mrs. Claus?"

My pajamas were silk and while they covered pretty much every part of me except my hands, feet and head, they were hardly conservative. I ignored him and went to placing some of my clothes into his gigantic walk-in closet. Despite my attempts to delay the inevitable, I completed the task quicker than expected. I took my time placing my toiletries next to his, but eventually finished the task. Finally, it was time for me to place my body next to his.

He was still reading his book when I came back. When I flipped open the linen on my side and climbed onto the bed, he didn't spare a glance at me. He seemed too engrossed by whatever he was reading to pay attention to me, which felt good at first, but after a while and when sleep refused to come, I became a little restless. Even the warm cotton sheets and the soft bed weren't enough to bring me to sleep. I turned around to see what he was reading. I had initially thought it was some business memoir or something boring like that, but on closer inspection, I realized it was fiction. An author I've never read, but one I had seen countless times in bookstores in the historical fiction section.

"I never took you for a World War two guy," I said.

"I'm not," he replied without lifting his head from the book.

"Interesting. So why are you reading a Churchill biography? One would be right to assume you're into World War two if they catch you reading the biography of one of the most influential men of the period."

"I thought it was fascinating when I saw it at one of the airport bookstores."

"And is it? Fascinating I mean."

He sighed and closed the book with a loud thud. He twisted his body to face me, and I rose slightly, mirroring his movements without thinking. "For someone who was nervous about sleeping here, you can be a little annoying once you warm up to the situation."

If I was not giving off nervous energy, then good because I was nervous as hell. Maybe that's why I couldn't stop talking. I wanted to shut up, but I couldn't. And now his naked torso was right in my eyesight. If he wanted to, he could lean over and at once cover my body with his. I would not protest. I could do the same too. Lean over to him and cover his body with mine and make him forget the old dude from the nineteen forties. Would he be willing? I bet he would. I could see it, him and I writhing against each other as we both slowly went mad with desire. Other images invaded my mind. Images of him with other women doing the same thing. They tormented me until I could not take it anymore. Out of the blue, I blurted, "How many women have you slept with in this bed?" I didn't mean to say it, but once it was out, I wanted an answer. For my sanity, at least.

The question surprised Gio. He regarded me with an inquisitive look. "Do you really want to know?"

How many were they? Ten? Twenty? Hundred? My mind would not rest until I got an answer. I nodded.

"Zero."

I scoffed. Even the most naïve person in this city knew it wasn't true. Not with his reputation. "Sure," I said. "And I'm the queen of England."

"It's true. I've never slept with anyone on this bed." He said so matter of fact that I was incapable of telling whether or not he was fooling around. I held his gaze to see if he would break the facade, but he didn't. I broke first. "Next, you're going to tell me you were a virgin the first time we had sex and have remained celibate until we got married."

"I never said I've never had sex. Nor did I say I've never brought a woman here. I've just have never had sex with anyone in this bed."

I was about to question how that was possible until I realized that he's had sex with me multiple times and I live here, yet we have never done it in his bed, or any other bed. If he were telling the truth, then he certainly had an odd kink. What was so special about his bed that he didn't want anyone in it? I asked him that. It took a while for him to respond. One would think I had asked something he had never contemplated before, which made even less sense considering it was an odd rule. Finally, he said,

"I hate cuddling."

"Why? Everybody loves cuddling."

"Not me. It's too intimate."

There was a time when he enjoyed it. When we slept together for the first time on his yacht, it had been in the bedroom of the main cabin and we had cuddled. I remember it well because I don't think I've ever felt that feeling of belonging to someone before or since. It had not only felt nice; it had felt right. Had that night on the yacht had something to do with his rule? I didn't want to find out. I might learn I'm the reason he's broken, and we had only started being nice to each other.

18

GIOVANNI

Simona was still sound asleep by the time I was done showering. She looked so beautiful in her sleep I didn't want to wake her, so instead I pressed a small kiss on her forehead. I was about to give her another until I realized what I was doing and stopped. We had agreed to be cordial, not loving. The issues between us were still there after all, and pretending that every problem had disappeared was foolhardy. And besides, our agreement was going well so far. Why ruin it with useless intimacy? That was not how I operate and it would confuse things between us now that I had destroyed a long held boundary; No sleeping in bed.

Technically, I hadn't broke the rule because all we did was sleep, literally. Not that it was a peaceful night. Knowing that Simona was an arm's reach from me and that I could just pull her to me, kiss her senseless and make love to her tormented my mind the entire night I hardly slept. By five am, I was tired of tossing and turning, counting sheep and looking at the ceiling that I got out and went to the gym. The workout provided some relief, but upon returning, I noticed the sheets had partially covered her body, and her pajama top had slipped up, revealing her alluring stomach, which immediately reignited my desire. One tiny movement and I could see her breast, I thought. Before I could succumb to the urge, I rushed to the shower and took a cold one. My boner didn't let up. I was still hard, so the next best thing was to let my thoughts go there and jerk off to the prospect of stripping off—no ripping off those offending pajamas and suck her rosy nipples until she screamed for me to stop. Then moving on to her lips and kissing while I drove deep into her warm heat. I jerked off so hard I came in record time.

And now fully dressed in a suit and tie, I was

still in the mind of fulfilling my shower fantasy. It was pathetic, really. Pathetic and unfair. She slept soundly while her mere presence tormented me. If she knew this was how she made me feel, she would not doubt have power over me. And who knew how she would use it? It was something I was determined she should never learn. That and the fact that she was the reason behind my rule. That night on the yacht, I completely surrendered to her. I've never behaved like that with anyone and that turned to have disastrous results. I shook away the memory. Better to focus on the present than the past, I thought.

Allison was already awake and in the kitchen when I got there. Brita was helping her make coffee and they only belatedly noticed my presence. "How did you sleep?" I asked Allison as soon as she saw me.

"Like a log of wood. That pill you gave me works like magic."

"Good," I said and waited for Brita to leave. Once she was gone, I continued the conversation. "And your wounds? How do they feel?"

"The eye hurts a little, but it will survive. Tell your wife she's a natural healer," she said.

"If I could crush that man, I could."

"Thanks, but I don't want you to. I want it to end. And dragging him through the courts would only be another form of harassment he would inflict on me. He hates to see me win."

"There are other ways I could deal with him," I said, and she quickly caught my meaning.

"I just want to let it go. I doubt he would do anything once he knows who I'm with. His family is smaller than yours and if they knew he did this, they would fuck him up."

She had gone through a lot and it was understandable if she wanted to let it go, but doing nothing made me feel helpless. Ever since she came back, I've been wondering if her initial visit had something to do with her trying to flee her boyfriend. She had been a little reserved, and I felt she wasn't saying more than she should. Maybe it was a relationship with Simona that complicated things. According to Simona, Allison hadn't told her she knew me, even though she had gotten several cues that Simona and I were together. Simona thought Allison was being duplicitous and what did she call it? Pulling a fatal attraction? It was an odd accusation. One I had a tough time agreeing with. The truth was much more likely to be more innocent than that. I also wouldn't be surprised if it had something to do with her situation.

"If you ever change your mind, know I'll be there for you," I said.

Allison nodded. "I've never doubted that for a second," she said. "You were very protective when we dated. I don't know…" She lowered her eyes. "Carter was the same at first. Just like you. Protective and sweet. And I liked that about him. And unlike you," she lifted her gaze to face me, "he seemed serious." I felt a pang in the pit of my stomach. "Allison…"

"I'm not saying I wanted you to be serious. I knew what I signed up for when we got together. I'm not saying that. It's just that I thought Carter would give me what was missing from our relationship and instead he gave me bruises. Your maleness led me to let down my guard and forget other less savory forms of maleness."

"Are you saying I ruined you?"

She chuckled, and I was glad she understood my joke. Then she quickly turned serious and said, "I guess you did." Her voice was low when she spoke and the distance between us was significantly less than before. Were we standing this close all along, or had she been tentatively moving forward? I stepped back, feeling uncomfortable at the intimacy.

"It's time I get to work," I said. Something about our conversation had shifted, and I didn't like it. An odd sense of guilt had grabbed me and wasn't letting go. "If you have any issues, don't hesitate to call," I added, and left.

I got to the office earlier than usual, ready to start the day. My conversation with Allison was still on my mind and I was willing to respect her wishes, but I still wanted to help her. Maybe if I look into the Carter guy and dig up some dirt on him, that might help her in the future if she ever thought of doing something. My private investigator was first on my schedule and he was already by my office when I came in.

"Come on in, Lewis," I said as I marched past, entering my office. I heard only the sound of the door closing. When I finished taking off my coat and starting my computer, Lewis had already seated himself on the chair opposite my desk.

"Found anything?" I asked him. Lewis was never one for pleasantries, so I never wasted his time with them. His face was sour when I asked him, and he didn't look like he had any new information.

"I found something."

"And?"

He took out his notepad and placed it on the table. Looking into Simona after last night's truce felt like a violation, so I made a mental note to tell him to end his investigation into her. Lewis cleared his throat, flicked through his notes looking for a page and then said, "We found three storages."

"Three?" How many clothes does she have that would need to be fit into three storages?

"One in her name and two others in the name of her assistant. She's not storing away any money or drugs, if that's what you were worried about. The storages are mostly for clothes. I even had one of my guys break in to see if there was any money underneath, and I can assure you there was nothing."

"I'm doubting if you're still as good as you used to be or you're losing your grip," I said. "I never asked you if she was hiding any money. It's the clothes I wanted you to follow."

Lewis's face contorted into animated confusion, the most emotion I've ever seen him display, before righting it back to its default sour state. "We did. She gives them away."

"What do you mean? As in donates them?"

Lewis nodded. "She works with a charity that provides clothes to people in developed countries. The um," he gazed down at his notes and flipped through a couple of pages, "The Dress The World Foundation. It's run by a woman in—"

"She's giving away clothes?" This was the last thing I expected to hear. The Simona I knew was selfish and prioritized herself above others. And if she was working with a charity, she would have shouted from the rooftops about what a great person she is for doing so.

"And these clothes are all hers?"

"Some are. Some not. My assumption is that some of her employees also donated to the cause on her insistence."

The image of Simona doing a charity drive failed to compute still. She was selfish, not altruistic. She was greedy, not giving. At least that's what I've seen so far. I guess there was a lot about my wife I didn't know.

"So this charity. How long has she been working with them?"

"The specific time frame? I don't know. From what I've gathered, though, it seems like she's been working with them for a while. I could look into it more…"

I shook my head. "That's enough for now. I want you to look into someone else." I told him about Carter and Allison. "See what dirt you can get on him," I said and dismissed him. Lewis marched out, leaving me to my thoughts.

Was it possible that I had judged her harshly? I didn't want a world where Simona was the injured party and I was a brute. If that world existed, what else was true and what else was a lie? That she didn't steal my money? That part was genuine enough. She didn't admit it, but she came close to admitting it when she told me of her pimp, handler, whatever that guy was she worked with. A niggling sense of doubt crept up in my mind and took hold. I could not let it go, try as I might. What if there was more to the story?

19

SIMONA

I came back home to the sound of laughter. It was odd hearing Gio laughing with someone else in our home. Well, his home. I should never forget that. I found Allison and Gio on the floor of the living room looking very comfortable with each other. That now familiar jealous bug rose again, and I gulped it down before it took over. Allison had an enormous book in her hand that they were both flipping through it with equal fascination while a bottle of wine and two half-filled glasses were forgotten on the table. Say what you will about my relationship with Gio, but we've never been this cozy before. I don't think we would ever be. I felt a pang in the pit of my stomach.

A scene like this would have made me throw some caustic remark to dampen the mood, but ever since last night's truce and Allison's revelations, acting like that would only be an unwarranted bitch move. So instead, I mustered up my best casual voice and said, "What have you two been up to?" They both looked up at the same time, startled, but the amusement of whatever joke they were sharing still lingering on their lips.

Allison lifted the book she was holding. "You will not believe what I found in this guy's study." It was a black book with gold lettering the size of a typical coffee-table book. "Our yearbook!" I swear she squealed when she said that. Our yearbook. They went to the same school. It made sense they had known each other that long. No wonder they were cozy. I glanced at Gio, who immediately launched into a rambling explanation when he noticed my puzzled expression. "Allison and I went to the same school for a like a year."

"Year and a half," Allison interjected. "I transferred mid semester, remember?"

"Oh yeah," Gio said, "Mr. what's his name? Our chemistry teacher made me your lab partner and practically forced me to get you up to speed with everything we had done."

"You were such a drill Sergent." They both laughed, clearly sharing an in-joke I was not privy to. A familiar sense crept in. Like I was a third wheel. An intruder. I brushed the feeling away. It wasn't fair to them or me for me to feel this way when there was clearly nothing going on between them excepted friendship. A wonderful friendship I must admit, if they can go through all they went through and still come out as friends. I should respect that. Allison had explained herself and Giovanni… well, he didn't so much as explain but show me his feelings last night. Last night was different for us. It was the first time we've ever had sex that wasn't just mechanical. It wasn't lovemaking, I don't think one would call it that, but it was closer. We came together in the middle of the night without meaning to. Our limbs touched, then our lips and the next thing I knew, Gio and I were exploring each other's bodies. I didn't wear my pajamas that night, and the dress I had on slipped off easily. When he took my breast to his mouth, I gasped. I moaned when he entered me. And when his cock stroked inside me bringing me to ecstasy, I screamed. He hasn't opened up to me, not yet, but he has shown a willingness to want to do so, so why not let him?

Instead of storming off upstairs or to the kitchen where I could hear chef Pierre preparing a meal, I instead threw my bag on the sofa and joined Allison and Gio on the floor. "I'm curious to see how he looked like as a teenager," I said to Allison. "Did he have any braces? Big nerdy glasses?"

Allison flipped back a few pages and stopped at a page where a row of students were pictured. She pointed to a tall boy at the back looking all broody and serious wearing evening wear, just like everyone in the image. "Sadly, he has never been ugly. Every girl at school wanted to date him."

"You were very handsome," I said to Gio. He smiled in return, as if he already knew that would be my response. What a cad. "And where are you?" I asked Allison. I scanned the image and couldn't see her or anyone who looked like her. She pointed to a girl wispy looking girl at the end of the row, taller than most people surrounding her. "I was the nerdy one, unfortunately. I didn't wear glasses, but had a mouth full of braces." My gaze went to her face out of curiosity. She was right. Seeing her now, you could not have guessed that it was the same person barring the height. It was not as if she had any work done. If she did, she had a good doctor. Her beauty was natural. A late bloomer.

"It must be nice to still be friends with people you met in high school," I said to them both.

"Oh, no. We weren't friends. At least not until college," Gio said. Allison looked a little startled by his response, but she nodded in ascent. I felt a prickling sensation at the back of my neck. A warning? I could not tell. Our conversation so far had been wholesome, so why was I getting the feeling that I should chuck her out of the window again?

A cloud of unease had since entered the room and hung over us. I could not think of anything else to say and Allison looked a little embarrassed, although why she was, I could not tell. She shifted awkwardly and her gaze kept darting between Giovanni and me. Meanwhile, I was at a loss at this sudden change in mood and didn't know what to say or do. Gio was the only one who seemed unbothered. And it was he who broke the silence. "How was your day?" he said to me. "Did I ask that? I feel like I didn't." Gio had never wondered how or what I was up to during the day unless I was somewhere I shouldn't be. However, I wasn't going to be the dampener and throw his small talk back in his face like I would have done before. Especially if there was someone else around. "It could have been better. The carpenters messed up the setup we were going for and they have to redo it. However, they want me to pay double the cost even though they're the ones at fault. And now they've refused to work until I pay the job, well, terrible job that they did."

"That sucks," Allison said. "What are you going to do?"

"Might as well pay them if I want the grand opening to be on schedule," I shrugged. "What can I do?"

Gio leaned forward, shifting from a relaxed state to one of anger. "Not let them roll you over. Do they know who you are?" I was a little taken aback by his reaction. He had never shown an interest in what was happening at the store and for his first reaction to be one of anger was a little heartening, even if it was a put on.

"It's not like I go around telling people what you do."

"What's the name of the company?"

I rattled off the name. He got angrier when he heard it.

"Give me your phone."

"What are you going to do?"

"Call them," he said casually.

"Then what? It's not as if they'll listen because you're my husband."

"Wanna bet?"

I glanced at Allison, who was listening to the conversation with interest. Gio and I were already making a scene, and I didn't want it to go any further, but I also didn't want to ruin the strained relationship I had with one of my contractors. "Call them on your own phone," I said.

"Fine." He whipped it out, punched a few keys and put the phone on speaker. Unlike me when I call them and it rings until it almost cuts, Gio only got two rings before it was answered. "Morelli!" A man said on the other end, "To what do I owe the pleasure?"

"Nothing, Benny," Gio replied. "I just have an issue with your employees." Benny was not a name I've heard of before, but I had a suspicion he was above all the people I've been dealing with.

"Your new apartment block? Something wrong with it? I was sure I sent my best men over there."

"No." He mentioned the address of my store. Benny sounded like he didn't recognize the name at first, but after a few clicks and typing noises he said, "That. I didn't know you were investing in single stores."

"Not me Benny, my wife."

"Oh," he chuckled. "I didn't know you had one. Is this recent? Uh, congratulations?"

"Thanks. Back to the issue. Sounds like your men are trying to stiff my wife. They refused to redo a mistake and asked her to pay double. Really, Benny, when has a Morelli ever paid twice for the same job?"

Benny chuckled again, nervously this time. "My people would never do that. It's just," there was typing, clicking and shuffling of papers in the background that gave the impression he was scrambling for an answer. "It's just protocol, that is all."

"Is stiffing your clients protocol Benny?"

Benny huffed. "Why would you say that? You wound me when you talk like that."

"You know, there are a lot of other contractors in the city. Some eager and cheaper than you are."

The line went quiet. I was sure it was dead until Benny cleared his throat and in the voice similar to that of a used car salesman he said, "And you would never go to them because we offer you — I mean you and your wife excellent service. I'm going to make sure this issue is rectified."

"You better. And Benny?"

He went quiet again. "Yes," he said after a few seconds.

"Send my wife better people next time," Gio said before ending the call.

I was gobsmacked. "That's it?"

"You can expect them to come to your store tomorrow. You might get a new team, though."

"That's even better. Thank you."

"You shouldn't let them roll you over," he said, as if it was the easiest thing to call who I assume was the head of the company I had hired and make them bend to my will. Even Allison looked impressed. For the first time, I truly felt the privileges of being a Morelli and, I had to admit, it felt good.

We had dinner inside this time around, and Chef Pierre joined us at my behest. Not because I was afraid of third wheeling again, but because I thought it awkward for us to eat a meal he prepared while he stood staring. And because he was good company. He had lots of culinary tales, mostly of kitchen mishaps and food related accidents, but was quite a well-traveled man. He regaled us with tales from his travels in Asia and Europe and that one time he had to cook for a family that reunited after a decade at the fall of the Berlin wall. Even Allison, who never seem to tire of interjecting or taking the conversation into a story of her own, sat back enthralled. Gio also was a different man. He was listening, yes, but he kept his gaze on me the entire duration of our supper, to where it was becoming unnerving. He took part in the conversation, yes, but I was sure each time he spoke it was to either reply to something I said or ask me something. To anyone observing, it was normal behavior, but not to me. He was paying attention, and that is something he's never done. By the time supper and wine—because Chef Pierre insisted on wine after supper—was done, my little tipsy self was happy that I would no longer be under Gio's watchful gaze and instead retreat to the comfort of my room. But that was not to be.

"Where are you going?" Giovanni asked just as I was entering my room.

"To bed," I said, yawning. Gio merely stood in the corridor, hands in his pocket, waiting for me to see my mistake. "Fuck." I can't believe I had forgotten that I would sleep with him while Allison was staying here. I don't think I could handle being in the same room with him again. Alone.

Last night was awkward. I doubt tonight would be different. At least last night I wasn't feeling on edge and unbalanced. Tonight?

"What if Allison and I have a girls' night in?" I said.

"I'm not going to maul you," he said as he strolled past me and went to open his door where he stood inviting me in. "Besides, you and I have things we need to talk about."

"Things?" Whatever he was referring to sounded ominous. And could I say no? Probably, but I was curious to find out. With heavy feet, I entered the bedroom, and he closed the door behind me. For the first time that evening, we were alone. Giovanni did not share the same curious nervousness that I had. He threw the jacket he had in his hand on a nearby chair and removed his tie. Were we having sex? Is that what was happening? No. After throwing his tie in the same place he put his jacket, he went to sit on the bed facing me, arms crossed.

"You never told me why you did what you did?"

"The story I was telling during dinner. I don't think there's much expla—"

He shook his head. "I'm talking about the theft. Why you stole money from me."

His gaze was scorching. It was like being under

a spotlight in a sheer gown. "I thought I told you. I wanted it, so I took it." Even the lie didn't sound convincing to my ears and he didn't buy it.

"I mean the truth. If we're going to keep up with the truce, tell me what really happened."

Did he find out something? He was not above looking into people's pasts. If he could have me followed, I'm sure he had someone checking my background. "Why now?" I asked. "Why do you care what I say when you'd never believe me, anyway?"

"Let's just say some things aren't adding up when it comes to you and I would like to know the real you."

I let out a strained laughter. "So you are looking into me," I said it out loud without meaning to, and he didn't even look ashamed.

"I had to at some point, you know that."

"And what did your detective say about me?"

"I want to hear the truth from you," his voice was soft, almost coaxing. There were several feet between us, and yet it felt like he had whispered the words against my neck. He seemed sincere. His tone felt sincere. Should I tell him? I could keep on with the rouse and let him think the worst of me. He would continue to treat me suspiciously and, in turn I would guard myself from loving him. Except that's not what was happening, was it? These past few days have given me a glimpse of a different Gio. The Gio I used to know. Back in Santorini. Back when I thought our little relationship could develop into something more. Before it all burned to ash. Before he said those words. I could keep the rouse, but I was getting tired of acting. And who knows, after all these years, he might not believe me, anyway. So what was I worried about?

"Where should I begin?"

He tapped the bed. "The beginning."

I felt my heart pounding as I moved to sit next to him. My voice cracked a little as I began my tale. "My parents never got along. She left him when I was young. She was a second wife, and he soon got a third one soon after, so he never really cared about her. My mother didn't care about him as well, but she loved his money. So we would visit my father here and there whenever the money ran dry, until one day, he refused to see us. He turned us at the gates. I was sixteen when that happened."

"That must have been hard for you."

"Not really. That was a high point, to be honest. The worst was yet to come."

"Oh?" Gio said.

"My mother never held a job in her life. She has

always had to rely on her ability to attract men to fund her lifestyle. And her drug habit. The older she got, the harder it was to lure rich men. Whales, she liked to call them. So, she turned to me. Her younger, more nubile daughter."

Gio grimaced. "Don't tell me she—"

"Made me sleep with men for money? No, she never went that far."

"What about that man we met? Terry?"

"Terry was my mom's sometimes boyfriend. He didn't have money, but he had connections. He could get into places, hotels, country clubs, and so on. You could say he was something of a pimp, and if it weren't for my mother, he would have made me sleep with our marks. But she always made sure it never got to that. My job was to lure a guy to my room, put something in his drunk and wait till he passed out. Then either Terry or my mom would take his valuables. A watch or some cash in a wallet. We later improved the con to swiping money from bank accounts. It's easier than you think. Most people willingly give their pass codes without a second thought. And when they find out they've been conned by a barely legal teen, they're too embarrassed to call the cops."

"Jesus Simona." I don't think I've ever seen Gio as devastated as he looked now. He really looked like he felt sorry for me. It was heartening.

"When I met you that afternoon in Santorini, it wasn't because you were a mark, if that's what you're thinking."

"You don't have to explain yourself."

"No please. I've lied for too long. It's time I tell the truth for once."

Gio gave a perceptible nod.

"I was in Santorini because I was on a break. That part was true. So was the graduation bit. I took online lessons and earned my degree at an open university. I was really proud of my accomplishments. We had also recently netted a big catch, so I had some money to celebrate. Mom and Terry had come along too and looking back, maybe I should have gone on my own. Anyway, that's when you met me. It wasn't a because I hatched a plan to reel you in. I was genuinely interested in you and it was the first time I've ever been with a person without trying to calculate how much money they're worth and so on. But then…" Those few days Gio and I had together were so good. He made me feel like I was worth more than my looks. He desired me. Yes, that was obvious. But he also liked to pick my brain. Listen to me. Get to know me. It was refreshing.

"And then?" He asked.

"And then Mom found out about you. She saw

me coming out of your yacht and told Terry. They both thought you were my mark. You should have seen them. Mom was so proud that I had caught someone on my own. She even offered to let me keep more than the ten percent I usually got. I didn't want to do it. You have to know that."

Gio's jaw clenched. His face was blank. I could hardly tell if he believed me or not.

"I told them you weren't that rich at all. I tried to convince him you were working on it. They didn't believe it. Terry looked you up and found out what you did. He didn't know the Mafia stuff, but he knew you were some hot shot Wall Street guy. After that, it was hard to brush them off. My mother's cocaine habit had gotten worse at that point and money was running out faster than before." I took a deep breath as the memories of what those days were like came to mind. The chaotic and fast-paced nature of our time together was as rough as a roller coaster ride. Mom was either drunk or high. Terry was getting more abusive towards her and whenever he was angry, he would taunt her by saying he would leave her for me. It wasn't something that would happen, but it only made her spiral further.

"I didn't want to do it. You have to understand that. I didn't want to until…"

"Until what?"

"The call." It took time for him to realize what I was talking about, but when it finally dawned on him, his features hardened. "I heard you talking to someone on the phone," I said. "You were talking about me. Apparently, the person had seen me in the background of your last video call, or something I can't remember."

"Dante," he said. "I was talking to Dante, and he was taunting me. He wanted to know if I was with someone."

I want to laugh, but it came out as a scoff. "I would never forget what you told him." *She's just another slut.*

"Simona…"

"No, it's fine. I've been called worse before. But when you, of all people, called me that, it reminded me of who I was. I may not think of myself as a slut and I may have not slept with all those men, but what I did was worse. I stole. It reminded me that whatever I thought we had, it would never work. It was a holiday fling. I meant nothing to you. So I did what I do best, I stole."

20

GIOVANNI

Simona went into all the details of how she got my pass codes and how she wiped out my account while I was asleep. It sounded simple in hindsight and I had been reckless with the information I gave her, but all of that didn't matter. I couldn't get over one simple fact; she loved me. I don't know about now, but she definitely loved me then. And in a masterful boneheaded move, I ruined all of that with four simple words. *She's just another slut.* I told Dante that because I wasn't sure yet what my relationship with Simona was going to be. We had been together for a week and spent most of that time making love. It was a flame I was sure would burn out eventually. It didn't. Still hadn't. All I knew was I wanted something more with her. I wanted to come back to New York with her, but I wasn't ready to admit that to Dante, much less to myself. It was an ephemeral idea that quickly evaporated when I found out she stole from me.

"I didn't take my cut," Simona said. "I gave Mom my share. She wasn't even embarrassed to take it." Simona shrugged. "I don't care if you believe me or not, but that's the truth."

"I believe you," I blurted out.

Her eyes widened. "You do?"

I nodded.

"You have no idea how much I've wanted to hear that from you. You're my biggest regret. The entire thing felt so dirty I got out of the business after that. Terry wasn't happy, but with my mom spiraling, keeping us as a team was becoming harder anyway, so he left. My mother went back to beg my father for money. He funded her for a while, but even he gave up as well. After that, she vanished, and I only reconnected with her recently. She seemed contrite and ready to get clean. She wanted to go into rehab, and I wanted to make sure she got the best help money could buy. This time it was my turn to go to my father with a begging bowl in hand and guess what he placed in it?"

"A marriage contract?"

"I signed without a second thought. I was selling myself, but at least this time around it was for a good cause, right?" She smiled, and it quickly faltered. Her confession was the last thing I expected to hear. My life felt so privileged and cozy compared to what she had gone through. Then along came me with my desire to exact revenge on her.

"You must think I'm a monster," I said. "I continued the horrible experience life dealt you."

She shrugged. It came off more like a sad shrug than the aloofness she tried to portray. "You're not the worst person I've been with. I'm just glad you believe me. I thought you would throw me out of your room immediately after hearing what I had to say."

"It lines up, if I had to be honest. I had my man look into something else and he stumbled onto that Terry guy and your association with him."

She smirked. "I wonder what he told you."

"Not much. Only that you two knew each other, but have since gone your own separate ways." I had assumed Terry was one of her boyfriends, so I never looked any deeper into that relationship. I was afraid of the wrong thing. The thought made me uncomfortable. "I just wanna know," I asked. "Would you have told me anything? If I never confronted you?"

"If you were in my shoes, would you?"

Not with the way I treated her. Would I have believed her if she said all this the day after we got married? No. I would have laughed in her face. Looking back, it should have been obvious that something was not straight. She wasn't a good liar. She was the same Simona I met all those five years ago and yet I was determined to see someone else, something else, because of one thing she did. But had she said something in Santorini... "Why didn't you come clean all those years ago? I would have protected you."

She raised her eyebrows. "You hardly knew me. Why would you trust anything I say? If I said anything, you would have thought that to be a scam."

"I knew enough to hear you out."

"Maybe. But not after that call."

The call again. "I should have never said those words. What I meant was—"

"It's fine. You don't have to explain yourself. What we had was a classic holiday fling gone wrong." She walled herself off, I realized. She didn't want to pursue the topic further. It was fine. I myself was still reeling from everything she told me. All the mistakes I made because of what I thought she was came to mind. I should try to make up for that. But how? I could not think of a way to resolve the gulf that was in our relationship. Hell, I don't even know if she wanted to resolve it. Our truce was a tentative one and the only thing so far that allowed us to even have this conversation. One wrong move and it could all blow up. There are other things I could do. Other ways to make it up to her.

"What if," I started, not sure where I was heading. What if we made up? What if we start over? What if what? The words lingered in the air.

"You and I were never meant to be," she said, as if reading my mind. "Our roads crossed once in a blissful moment and should have never crossed again."

"You don't believe that, do you?"

"I'm not the woman you want to marry. If we didn't meet, you would have married someone else. Someone better."

"Who? Allison?"

"I've seen the way you two interact. You finish each other's sentences."

"That's because we've known each other for a long time. We're friends, that's it. I'm not in love with her Mona."

And just like that, the nick name tumbled out. I didn't even notice that I called her Mona until I heard her breath catch in her throat. I took her hand in mine and held in my lap. It felt soft in mine; I squeezed it gently. I love you. The words could not come out of my throat as much as I tried. And yet, the longer they turned in my head, the more sense they made. I love her. I've loved her ever since I met her and when I met her again, I fell in love all over again. Once I stopped fighting it, my heart felt like bursting. Even when I hated her, I loved her. I hated I was in love with her. And now? Now I want to scream it at her. At the city. At the world. But it didn't feel right to say it now. She would reject them and I don't think I could handle it.

"Mona," I said again, softly this time, "I want to make amends."

"You don—"

"I do. Please, let me."

She looked hesitant. Her mouth opened and closed before she finally nodded. I lifted her hand and kissed it. I wanted to do more, but not tonight. Not yet. Even Simona seemed surprised when I told her to change for bed. She didn't hesitate, though. She was just as, if not more, drained that I was. When she went to the closet,

I got up, left the room, and went to the office downstairs.

I had to leave her so I could take in all I had learned on my own and also to give her space. Our relationship had shifted, my head was reeling and earth had fallen off it's axis. A drink would be good, I thought when my gaze landed on the decanter on my desk. I poured a shot and gulped it down in two drinks. The fiery liquid burned down my throat and did little else to calm my nerves. What I needed was a plan. If there was one thing I was capable of was planning. I went over to the other side of the desk and sank into the chair. I had left my laptop on, which is something I didn't usually do, but there were so many things on my mind when I came back from work, I must have forgotten to put it on sleep. Luckily, the notes app was on screen. My hands were tingling with so much energy when I typed. Step one. Earn her forgiveness. How else would she believe me to be genuine if she hadn't forgiven me? It was going to be difficult to do, but it would require showing her I did not care about what she did before. That I had forgiven her. That one was going to be hard, and I had no idea how to do it.

On to step two. Woo her. That one was easy. Simona and I could go on a trip together.

Somewhere far from this place. This apartment was too tainted with hate. I needed somewhere pure where we could rediscover our love. Some beach somewhere were it could just be the two of us. Barbados or Seychelles. Dante had a private island off the coast of Spain. We could go there. Or we could… No. She would smack me if I took her there. My plan might unravel. But it might not. It was a risk worth taking.

Step three. Renew our vows. Hell, renew everything. The entire marriage was built on a foundation of hate. A new marriage would be built on love. If she forgives me. If I woo her. If she loves me back. The thought of not having my love reciprocated was difficult to stomach and if at the end of it all, she didn't love me the —

"Working late?" In my haste to jot down my plan, I didn't hear the door open, or anyone enter. I looked up to see Allison standing in the doorway wearing a nightdress. A sheer, white silk dress that stopped at her thighs.

"I thought you were asleep," I said. I'm sure I said it dismissively, but she seemed to take it as an invitation to enter. A little annoyed, I closed my laptop and leaned back in my chair.

"You don't have to stop on my account," she said, gliding over to my side of the desk.

"I wasn't working."

"This late? I know you, Gio. You can't fool me."

She was standing a couple of feet away from me now. She looked statuesque; I thought. Like a life-size doll. Pretty and cute at the same time. But not enough to tempt.

"If you thought I was working, wouldn't you want to leave me to it?"

"You have more than enough money. You don't need to work so late. Unless…"

I raised my eyebrows, not catching her meaning.

"Unless you're hiding from someone."

"My wife? I promise you I'm not."

"Again. Can't fool me as much as you try." She stepped forward and turned the distance between us from friendly to intimate. If Simona were to come in now, she might think something is going on, I thought. That's when I realized Allison had closed the door to the office. Her flimsy nightgown was also making me wonder about the purity of her intentions.

"My wife and I are happily married," I said, pushing back my chair a little. Unfortunately, the leg of the desk was on the way.

"Says the man who prefers looking at boring charts instead of being in bed with his newly wedded wife."

"What's your game here, Allison?"

"Game? I'm simply being upfront. You're the one who's faking. Faking your marriage. Faking your feelings, and who knows what else?"

Shit. Allison was smart, and I knew eventually she would have worked it out the longer she stayed here. I could continue the lie. Tell her it's real. But was it even a lie when I wanted it to be true? "What's it to you?"

"Friends look out for each other. I'm looking out for you as you did me. It's only natural, don't you think?" She lowered her voice to a sultry register. Her chest was almost in my face as she leaned towards me. She had nice breasts. Good looking breasts I've lusted after before. Now, however, they were a distraction. I turned my attention to her face. A small upturn of a smile was slowly forming. No, a smirk. She's trying to seduce me, I realized. And she thinks she's got me. If only it were that easy. The only person I was thinking of at that moment was Simona. Specifically, her reaction if she were to see us like this.

I leaned back to put more space between us. "It's late," I said. "You should go to back to bed."

"What if I don't want to?"

"You're free to roam in here and do whatever you want," I said, standing up. In order to do so, I practically had to push her out of the way. She was as rigid as a brick wall, refusing to budge. When she did, she moved in such a way that her chest brushed against mine. If this were Simona, I would have a raging boner right now. But with Allison, I was annoyed. "I'm going to bed."

"Don't." She grabbed hold of my hand and clasped it in hers.

"Allison." It was a warning. She did not heed it. Instead, she took my hand and placed it on her left breast. I snatched it away, repulsed by the mere idea. "I think you have gone too far." My voice was cold and hard. The kind of tone I reserved for people who were about to receive my wrath. For Allison's sake, I hoped at that moment she wasn't one of them. Smart as she was, she seemed to not take the hint.

"I have a wife," I pressed further.

"You don't love."

"What's between Simona and I is none of your business."

"I don't intend it to be. All I care about is you and I. Our relationship."

"We're friends. That's all we'll ever be."

"We were more before. We've always colored outside the lines." She brushed her hand down my chest. I caught it and swiped it away before she went any lower. Her smile faltered. "I'm not interested in you, Allison. I only want one woman and it's not you."

My words seemed to sink in this time. Instead of the tentative forward press she was doing, she stepped back and crossed her hands around her chest. A little surprised. A little shy. She took a huge gulp. Was she pushing back tears? I could not tell and I didn't care, to be honest. My annoyance was overriding any compassion I might have felt for her.

"Wow," she said finally, "You do love her."

I shrugged. It felt more like a statement of fact coming from her, and in a way, it kinda was.

"Why?"

Why do I love my wife, the only person who's ever held up a mirror to my face and showed me the real me? The only person who challenges me and isn't afraid to do so? What's not to love? There were so many reasons I could have told Allison, some of them I hadn't fully understood yet, but before I could say anything, she added, "Why her? Do you have any idea what kind of person she is?"

"I do. It might be why I love her, actually."

"You wouldn't say that if you knew—"

"That she used to be part of a team that conned people out of money? Yes, I was aware. She told me all of that." Technically, I didn't know all the details until tonight, but there was no reason to give Allison that information. Her face fell when she realized the most powerful weapon in her arsenal turned out to be a dud. She must have thought that this would be a surprise to me. And besides, even if I hadn't known, it was not as if I would have run into her arms. The more she tried to seduce me and smear Simona, the less attractive she became. Spite wasn't her color.

"And you're happy with that? A slut who would loves money more than you?"

"Careful Allison. That's my wife you're talking about."

Her eyes narrowed. She glared at me as if she was looking at me from a different perspective. A specimen she was seeing in a whole new light. And then, as if this new realization was too unreal, she shook her head and made another move. This time, her hand went to my waist. I was too slow to react and froze when she placed her lips on mine. The kiss was desperate and sad. It was only a millisecond before I removed her away from me.

"Allison," I started.

"You don't love her. You don't. You love me." Her voice was shaky with emotion. I don't know when or how it had happened, but somewhere along the way, she had deluded herself into thinking she was in love with me.

"It's Simona Allison. She's the one I care about. Now leave this office before you learn a side of me you don't want to know." She froze. My threat was clear. Tears welled in her eyes as the message sank in. "I want you gone tomorrow morning," I added. "My men will take you to one of my apartments in Brooklyn. I think you've overstayed your welcome."

21

SIMONA

I woke to the delicious smell of eggs, bacon, and coffee. Gio was sitting in bed beside me shirtless, but looking fresh with a tray in his hands.

"Eggs benedict?" I croaked as I sat up and straightened. My sleep had been easy to come by after last night's revelations. The weight I was carrying on back all these years was now off, and I felt light and tired. I don't even remember falling asleep, only waking up now to two meals. The first looked just as good as the second. A bright yellow poached egg was perfectly placed on top of a meaty turkey bacon and a fluffy English muffin underneath. The second dish, Gio himself, was smiling and had a welcoming warmth to him I hadn't seen in a while. Since before we were married. He was dangerously unassuming and sexy in a way that made me feel embarrassed to face him, just as I was waking up when he clearly had been up for some time.

"Thought I made you something before you went to work," he said.

"You did this?" The dish had Pierre's name written all over.

"No." Was that a blush? I don't think Gio was capable of reddening or feeling any embarrassment of some sort. "But I told Pierre to it make for you special."

"Why? What's the occasion?"

"Do we need one?" His eyes were hot and piercing as he stared at me. It made the overall combo a lot more unsettling than I would have wanted in the morning, especially after last night.

I cleared my throat. "If this is about last night and your guilt, you don't need to do this."

Gio shook his head. "It's not about guilt. I was serious about what I said last night. We should start anew. Well, brand new. No more fighting.

No more truces. After you went to sleep last night, I stayed up all night thinking, not just what you said, but what we've done to each other. We've hurt each other."

I nodded absentmindedly.

"We angered each other when we should have communicated. We've wasted so much precious time over trivial things."

"But I stole—"

"Money can be replaced. I already did it one hundred times over. It wasn't the money you took that made me angry. It was the betrayal. It was the hurt. The thought that the woman I—the woman I saw myself with could turn on me so easily is what angered me. And instead of getting to the root of that anger and what it could mean, I've wasted time trying to make you pay. Make you hurt the same way I was hurting. I want to change that. I want us to start over. To truly start over."

"Gio…"

He placed a hand on my thigh. "Don't. Please don't say no. At least think about it and give us a chance?"

I wanted it too. He had no idea how much I wanted it so badly. Giovanni Morelli is the only man I've ever wanted. The only man I've been with whose presence I've loved to be in. Even when he was kind. Even when he was hateful. I was that pathetic for him. And yet. I don't think I could do it again. He made a similar speech last night and in the light of the day, there still wasn't that much change between us. He was still Gio, and I was still Simona. As much as I wanted to believe that we could work out, we were still the same people. We both had a capacity to hurt each other, like he said. However, there was that small voice within me saying yes. Give him a chance. Give your relationship a chance.

"And Allison?" I asked. I hated being the jealous wife, but I could not ignore their relationship. They knew each other. Understood each other. Comfortable in a way I doubt Gio and I will ever be.

"Gone," he said.

My eyes widened without meaning to. "Back to her place? What about her boyfriend?"

"I found another place for her," he spat. He sounded angry, and I wasn't sure about what. "It's what I should have done from the beginning. We had agreed to work on our relationship and then I brought my ex into the mix. That was callous of me."

"She's my friend too, you know. As weird as that is. And she is going through a lot."

A dark cloud fell over his face. The change in

mood was as swift as it came, however, and it quickly went away. "It's better if she has a place of her own. Better for us as well if we are to work on our relationship. If you want that."

The statement hung in the air. Did I want it? The tiny yes voice was growing louder. What was there to lose? My heart. If it broke a second time, I don't know how I would recover. But if I never gave it a go, I would regret saying no till my dying breath.

"One month," I said. "One month where we explore our relationship. If doesn't work out, we divorce."

He winced. I hope he didn't expect us to stay married together if it didn't work out. We would make each other miserable if we stayed together for longer than that.

"One month is too short."

"It's enough to assess where we are."

"Fine. A month it is." He leaned forward and placed a kiss on my mouth. "It's about to become the best month of your life," he whispered.

I pulled back and looked down at the tray between us. "That breakfast better be the start."

Gio was right. The following month was one of the best times in my life. He was a man on a mission. His challenge; make me fall in love with him. And he was close to accomplishing the goal. Every day, he did something new. We did something new. We went out almost every night. And on weekends, he would take me to some unknown destination. Last week it was Paris. I had absently mentioned that I've never been to the Louvre, and the next thing I knew, he was taking me there. The other day we had got to talking about marine life and I mentioned the Galapagos. What do you know, come Friday evening, he was standing outside my store ready to take me there? I didn't say no. The trips were a great way of taking my mind off the looming store opening. So many things needed to be done and additional problems kept coming up. Gio had been helpful in that area. After the business with the contractors, Gio was now inquiring if they were keeping their end of the bargain. They were and had finished the work in record time.

It was odd seeing him caring about what I did for a living. Hell, last night he even came to the dress the world fundraiser as my plus one and left a large donation for the charity. How he knew I was a patron to a charity, I never got to ask because immediately after we got back, he scooped me up and took me to bed. His bed. We had never truly made love until that night. His kisses were sweet and tender. He was warm and generous. He made sure I came first and multiple times. Only when I felt breathless and boneless did he enter me and tortured me again to ecstasy. We came at the same time. Our bodies shook in an embrace so sweet I thought I was going to die. It was then I thought he was going to say the words. I was sure he was going to say I love you and it sounded like he said the first two letters, but it could have been a stutter. He had come down from an earth-shattering orgasm, after all. But two letters aren't three words. A tender kiss or a sweet caress was not a substitute for the real thing. If he loved me, I had to hear him say it. That way, I would know if he was telling the truth or not. Actions were hard to decipher. That was the problem. He said everything but those three words. His silence made me doubt him and, in turn made me doubt his intentions. He could be doing all this because he felt sorry for me. Because he wanted to keep the marriage intact.

And once again, he was wooing me. This time on an island off of the coast of Spain. It was a beautiful place. The beaches were gorgeous and were reminiscent of Santorini. The only difference between this place and the other one is that it was a lot more secluded. Giovanni and I were the only people to be received by the retinue of staff waiting for us when we arrived. It was peak summer and odd that it would be the island would be empty this time of the month. "Did you book the entire place," I asked as we headed to the hotel.

"In a way. Rio wanted to throw a party here, but I called dibs."

"Called dibs?" It didn't make sense at first until the implication of what he was saying sank in. "You're telling me this is your private island."

"Technically it's Dante's island, but it's actually the family island if you ask me. He rarely comes here while the twins practically live here. It's their favorite vacation spot."

I took in building we were entering and realized that it was not a hotel but a beach house. Was there such a thing as a beach mansion? This was it. It was grand but did not stand out against the nature and beauty surrounding it. It was beautiful inside just it was out. Sometimes it was hard to reconcile the wealth Gio had especially now that he was spending it like a mad man. Of course I should have guessed that he would be taking me to a private island. We were a jet setting couple now. I don't remember the last time I had flown to so many places in a short amount of time.

This place felt different though. Maybe it was the similarity to Santorini or maybe it was the exclusivity. It felt familiar and intimate.

We spent a few more days there than intended. At the end, I had to concede that the island was my favorite place in the world. Gio was a different person there. Not changed, just another perspective. He was more open, relaxed and very much like the Gio I fell in love with on Santorini. Our days were spent exploring the island. On top of a beautiful stream and a waterfall, the island also had a cave system that had beautiful dark blue pools. That was my favorite place of all. Our nights were just as active. His lovemaking was passionate and desperate. Like a man hungry for food that would never satiate him. And I loved it all. I didn't want to leave. On our last night I said as much. Gio and I were sitting on the terrace drinking wine while watching the sun sink into the ocean. His arm hung lazily around my shoulder while I laid my head against his chest.

"We don't have to," he said. "We could move here if you want."

I chuckled. "Your brothers will kill us for taking their party spot."

"I'm being serious. We can move if you want."

I scoffed. "Sure, Mr. Wall Street. I've seen you work. You love your job."

"Not as much as…" he trailed off.

I looked up at him. He was about to say something. He could say it, if he wanted to. "As?" I asked almost breathless.

His mouth curved into a sad smile. His hand caressed my arm and he drew me closer to him. Is he going to say it? I was sure he was about to say it before something shifted on his face. He frowned his features contorting into a pained expression. "I never meant what you thought I meant," he said.

I straightened but remained in his arms. "I feel like there's been a change in subject."

"When I said she's just a slut," he said.

"It's water under the bridge, we don't have to rehash it."

"I want to. You should know what I meant." He straightened in his seat as well. As much as I wanted to forget about that cursed end to our meeting, I could see I wasn't going to dissuade him from rehashing it. So I let him continue. "I was speaking to Dante. He had seen you in a previous call. I had delayed a meeting with him so I could spend more time with you. I was considering seeing you again. Taking you with me. Whatever it took to keep you close. Dante had no idea who you were but he guessed there was a woman who had changed me. I didn't get that yet. All I knew is that I wanted to be with you. So when he asked who you were, I didn't want to tell him the truth. That you were special. Thinking of you in that way scared me. I've never thought of anyone like that. So I said you were just another slut. Because I could not accept the truth."

My heart skipped a beat. "Which is," I asked.

"That I loved you. I loved you then. I probably loved you when I married you and I definitely still love you now. My love for you is an unshifting constant that I've fought against from the moment I met you. Fought every minute I was with you and now I'm realizing how silly that is. How stupid. I love you Simona. Even if you don't. And I'm tired of fighting it."

22

GIOVANNI

I had said the words. I don't know what I thought would happen after I told her the truth. It's not as if she could just say I love you too and everything is forgiven. As much as I would love that. No. She's not going to accept me yet, but I could tell the ice around her heart was thawing. She didn't say anything, however her eyes said a lot, and that was enough for now. Our trip to Dante's island changed things. We were closer than before. Simona was more open. Our relationship was getting better. My plan is working, and I was loving every single step. It meant spending time with her, which honestly was the best part about the entire thing. Hell, I was looking forward to coming home every day. The sex, too, was fucking amazing. I constantly found myself lost inside her every time we made love. And we were doing it often. And somehow not enough.

After we came back from Spain, I thought Simona would be tired or would not want to be with me after my confession, but when I kissed her goodnight; she continued the kiss until I forgot. We both forgot it was supposed to be a simple kiss. We did it right there in the foyer. Our bodies were tired, but the lust was so overpowering that we languidly removed our clothes and slid down onto the floor, where we explored each other's bodies until we reached climax. We both passed out and then later I carried her and took her to bed.

This morning, the same thing happened. A simple kiss spiraled into passionate lovemaking and we both ended up being late for work. And now that I was at work, I was thinking about her instead of doing my job. I focused on the screen I had been staring at for half an hour. I loved my job, and yet right now I found the numbers and graphs dreary. Maybe I should call it a day. It was only midday and my heart wasn't in it. Maybe I should visit her store. She had been preparing for the opening and our time in Spain might have taken away time from her work. I sent her a text asking her if she wanted to any help. Her response came in a few minutes later.

"Don't you have work to do?"

"All I see on my computer screen are your tits. I've given up," I responded.

She sent a blushing and a laughing emoji.

"I'm coming over." The text was delivered, but I didn't check to see if she had seen it. I had already placed my phone in my pocket and was preparing to call it a day.

"I'm leaving," I said to my assistant when I got out of my office.

"You had a meeting with Mr. Lewis. He is coming over."

"Schedule it for tomorrow and everything else I have today."

Her mouth gaped. She could not hide her shock. I rarely left the office during the day. It felt odd for me to leave this early as well. "You're leaving for the day?" she asked.

"Yes. Is that surprising?"

"N-no," she stammered.

The elevator dinged, the doors opened, and

Lewis came through. My assistant glanced between the two of us, unsure what to do. She looked like a petrified bird. I took her out of her misery and said to Lewis. "I was heading out. Let's reschedule."

"I have found out some information you might want to know," he said.

My heart skipped a bit. "About Simona?"

He shook his head. "But I think you might want to hear it."

"Fine," I said. I went over to the elevator and pressed the button. "Tell me on the way down."

"It's about Allison," he said as soon as we entered the elevator.

"What did you find out?"

"It's not good. Remember the boyfriend she was running away from? Turns out she doesn't have one. It's a friend."

"Her friend beat her up?"

"No. Well yes."

"You're not making any sense. Lewis."

Lewis turned to face me. "It's a long story, but basically my guys had been trying to track down this Carter guy you told us of. He was pretty elusive. Turns out, dude never existed."

"She made him up?"

"Yes, and no." He raised a finger. "Carter does not exist, but a friend who beat her up does. I can't prove it definitively, but I think her friend beat her as part of a ruse."

"Whatever for?"

"That part I don't know, but she came to your place battered and bruised, didn't she?"

If he was suggesting that Allison got herself beat up to in order to gain sympathy from me, then he must have missed something or gotten something wrong. For all of Allison's faults, deceit wasn't one of them. She was up front about everything. Hell, my last night with Allison was proof of that. "She did, but I don't think she was making it up. What would be the point?"

Lewis tilted his head to the side as if to say I was wrong. "We also found out she has been stalking your wife."

"The fuck?" The elevator came to a halt at that moment and the doors opened, but I made no move to get out. Lewis, who was less shaken than me stepped out. I followed him as we made the way to my car. Johnny was already standing by the door.

"Allison has been seen near your apartment and your wife's store by my men several times."

"That doesn't mean she's stalking Simona. They're friends."

"I personally saw her several times, spending hours at a time in a car parked directly across the street from where Mrs. Morelli's shop is and not bothering to interact with her. Instead she was scoping the place with a pair of binoculars. She would also follow Mrs. Morelli's car."

I still could not believe what he was saying. Stalking. Creeping from afar. It did not sound like the sophisticated and aloof Allison I knew. She's never cared about the people I've been with before. Was it because of what I said? "Do you have any idea when this started?"

"From what I can find, immediately after you got married."

We had reached the car by now, and Johnny was opening the door. I stopped, shocked at what he was saying and the implications behind that statement. Had I missed something when it came to Allison? I had taken Johnny and removed him from Simona's retinue. She had complained about having two men following her around. She said it made her feel like a mobster. I wanted to please her, so I had relented, but I insisted she keep Mickey. I prayed I had not made a fatal mistake.

"Is she still stalking her?" I asked.

"Not recently," Lewis said.

Maybe she gave up after I kicked her out of the apartment. Maybe she finally got the hint. "Thanks Lewis. Stay on Allison," I said to him and got into the car. "Take me to Simona's store," I told Johnny. He nodded and got into the driver's seat. I took out my phone and called her. I called her three times, but it kept going to voicemail. Don't panic, I told myself. It might mean nothing. Simona was busy, after all, and she might not have her phone next to her. And for all I knew, Lewis might be wrong. The Allison he painted was not the Allison I knew. She wasn't some obsessive person who would try to harm my wife. Right? That night in my office came to mind. But that was probably my fault. I was the one who gave her the wrong impression, and that's why she reacted the way she did. My phone dinged. A message popped up. Simona? It was Lewis. "I forgot to tell you. Allison's friend. It's Leonardo."

23

SIMONA

I shouldn't have let them in. It was stupid of me to do so. When I saw them together, I thought something was off, but I ignored the warning bell ringing in my head and instead opened the door. Besides, while no one else had come to the store, employees or contractors, I wasn't alone. Mickey was with me and he was at the back arranging the shoe inventory that had come in.

"Fancy place," Leo said as he walked in, Allison immediately behind him. The contractors had finished all the interior decor, and the rococo inspired style I was going for really came out. It had been a hassle, but the finished product looked good. All that was left was the inventory and it would be a shop.

"Surprised to see you two—" I never got to finish the sentence. Leo went behind me and whacked my head with something hard. Then I was falling. My vision failing. The last image I saw was a creepy smile on Allison's face. It all faded to black after that.

I woke to the feeling of hard cold tiles against my cheek and the ache in my hip and arm muscles. I slowly tried to stretch my legs, but a restraint made the act impossible. Someone had restrained my hands, too. Bound behind my back. My legs were bound around my ankles. Moving only made the aches worse. I winced.

"She's up," a voice said. Leonardo? "Let her go," the voice said again. No. Not Leo. Giovanni. I tried to get up and sit straight, but it was difficult to do when hands and ankles are bound. I heard footsteps on the floor and then saw Giovanni rushing towards me. "Stop!" Allison cried out. Gio ignored her and helped me sit. He brushed my hair off my face, helping me see clearly. "It's going to be okay, my love." Gio looked relieved. His face was pale and haggard.

As if he had aged years in a few seconds. There was blood on his shoes. And some on his jacket. What happened? Whatever it was, I was happy to see him.

A weary smile crossed my face.

"I said stop!" Allison screamed again. I saw Gio's face go from happy to angry to sad in mere seconds. "Let us go Allison," he took me into his arms placed me onto the counter, but did not let me go. Oh god. Oh no. There were pools of blood all over the white marble floors. There were shell casings and worse. Bodies. Mickey was unconscious or…dead. No. It can't be. He was in the storage a few minutes ago. Or was it a few minutes? Time had passed since I blacked out and a lot had happened. Leonardo was lying motionless in his own pool of blood a few feet away. Between them, Allison stood with a crazed expression in her eyes and a bloody gun in her hand. I clung to Gio. "Let us go and I will tell no one what happened here. I can even make all of this go away. I can give you money. You can start a new life somewhere and we can pretend any of this never happened."

Allison shook her head. Her eyes were bloodshot and swollen. Her once immaculate mascara running down her cheeks. "Not without you. I can't stand the thought of you being with that slut! Do you know? She's a slut who sleeps with men for money and you choose her over me?" She shook her head again. "No. She has to die."

I felt Giovanni's arms tighten. "Give me the gun," he said and extended a hand.

"No," she said in a small voice and pointed it at me. Time seemed to slow down. Each second passed like a minute. Allison clocked the trigger. She sniffed. A shot. I closed my eyes, expecting the bullet to hit me. I fell down on to the counter. Gio was on top of me. Blood pooled. My blood or his blood? It was hard to tell. Another shot. I heard a body crumble to the floor.

I heard Gio groan, and I opened my eyes. He winced in pain. No. No. No. "She shot you." I could barely get the words out. They were whispers between tears. "Don't die." Gio smiled it was weak and sad. He shook his head. "I'm not going to." He gave me a slow, wet kiss and pulled back. His arm was wet with blood. I heard another groan and my gaze went to the floor. Mickey was leaning on his arm. In his other hand, he had a gun pointed at Allison, who lay crumpled on the floor. Mickey was alive. But Gio. Gio straightened and grimaced, but pulled through the pain as he looked all over me. "I'm not hurt," I said. He smiled. "Good. That's all that matters."

I later learned all about Allison from Gio. Not only had she been stalking me ever since that day in the park, she had convinced Leo into a wild scheme where they would both kidnap me and she would convince Gio I had run away with Leo. Apparently, she had paid Leo a large sum for him to agree to this. The only snag was Mickey. Mickey and Gio. They didn't think he was there at the shop and thought I was alone. If it weren't for Mickey, who came in after hearing a commotion, who knows what might have happened. Mickey has seen Leo and immediately thought something was fishy. When he saw me lying on the floor, he pulled out his gun. Leo did the same, and they shot each other. Gio came to the shop while Johnny was looking for a parking spot. He saw all the chaos and tried to intercede to no avail. Luckily for her, she didn't die. The bullet had hit none of her essential organs and had passed cleanly through her body. Gio had only been grazed on his arm and Mickey had a leg injury. Leo was the only one to die.

To think Allison's plan might have worked. Allison would have dripped lies into Gio's ears and he might have believed him. When I said this to Gio, he choked with laughter. "I would have searched for you to the ends of the earth," he said. "I wouldn't have believed her. Not after finding out she had injured herself just so she could gain sympathy points from me."

That was another shocking revelation. Allison's plan had initially been just to worm her way into our lives by pretending she had an abusive boyfriend who beat her up. She had hired Leonardo to beat her in a way that would cause bruises but not hurt too much. When that didn't work, she went on to plan B.

Insane as the entire situation was, it made me realize one thing. As I spent time in hospital beside Gio, watching over him, it all became clear. I had almost lost him. He could have died. He took a bullet for me and he could have died. The thought was unbearable. When he was discharged from the hospital and we got back home, that's the first thing I said to him. We were in the bathroom and I was dressing his wound according to the nurse's instructions. "You could have died," I said after I was done.

Gio smiled. "A happy death, if it meant you were alive."

"Don't say that. You have no idea how I would have felt if you were gone."

"Tell me," he whispered. "How would it have felt?"

"Lonely. Depressing. A colorless existence. Don't you dare make me contemplate that thought? I love you too much to even think about the possibility," I said.

With his other hand, he drew me to him until my body was plastered against his. "Say that again."

"What? The part about life being a dreary experience without you?"

"No," he said against my lips. "The other part."

I smiled. "I love you too much…" I never finished the statement. He ended it with a kiss.

The end.

ABOUT THE AUTHOR

Piper Knox has always had a passion for romance stories ever since she heard her first fairytale. She started writing when she was thirteen and has not stopped. She's fueled by coffee and often distracted by either one of her two cat overlords. When she's not writing, she's reading or baking experimental cookies.

Printed in Great Britain
by Amazon